To Birdie ~

I hope you have fun with this story!

Her Secret Santa

By Bonnie Engstrom

This book is dedicated to my long time friend from high school, Sandy Cervi Bacasa, who inspired this story by playing Mrs. Santa and never colored her stunning gray-white hair. She is a beautiful woman and a perfect Mrs. Claus.

Special Thanks To

My Lord and Savior Jesus who gave me the courage and energy and faith to write stories. I pray you enjoy them, and I pray He does. I hope He is singing over this one.

The LORD your God is with you, he is mighty to save. He will take great delight in you, he will quiet you with his love, he will rejoice over you with singing. Zephaniah 3:17(NIV)

Author Alice Arenz who prayed me through this story. I printed out her prayer and it's sitting beside my keyboard. What would authors do without other authors? Alice is the best. I hope you read her wonderful award-winning stories.

Author Kimberly Grist who graciously critiqued my Santa story and gave me encouragement. I hope you read her lovely stories.

Author and special friend Tanya Eavenson who is always in the background supporting me and doing the dull and boring tasks of my promotions. I hope you will read her wonderful books.

Neighbor Julie Gutteridge who told me the true story about how her sister's husband passed away suddenly and gave me an interesting scene about dying suddenly.

All the wonderful friends I've met who support me by commenting on my Facebook author page and in emails. You are all precious to me.

Dave, husband extraordinaire, who makes yummy dinners and patiently holds them when I am writing or editing and also advises me about psychological stuff. He's a Ph.D. shrink ya know.

Cynthia Hickey, publisher and friend, who designs outstanding book covers and is patient with my writing. Only because of her have I written and published fifteen books.

One

ONE

"I need a job." Patti pressed her nose against the vanity mirror. "Don't you think?" The mirror didn't answer, but she kept talking to her reflection. "Just a part time one for over the holidays. Yes," she nodded, "that would be perfect. But where? Who is going to hire me, an older woman with gray hair?" She refused to call herself old. Older would do.

She dug through the recycle trash basket and pulled up crumpled newspaper. Where was yesterday's? She finally found it. The Thursday Arizona Republic was the issue that had a lot of job listings. Spreading it out on her kitchen counter she ran her finger down the few listings for part time holiday work. They were all for retail. Nope, not any more. She was over the demanding hours, especially at Christmas time.

In her younger days she'd had to be at Casual Corner at 6:30 a.m. to be ready for when the shop opened at seven. At least if she was organized she could nurse her cup of coffee while customers lined up outside the door. As the designated key-carrier she was responsible for unlocking and opening the heavy glass door. She remembered pulling it in front of her and standing behind it for protection. People who shopped that early were always in a frenzy. There were more than a few pushers and elbowers. Not a pleasant crowd for the most part. They dug through the sale merchandise, dropping some to the floor and shoving clothes haphazardly on the racks. Nope, no more fashion retail in this life.

Her finger stopped on an ad for the local Hallmark gift shop. Not the same kind of retail that she despised. She loved the merchandise it carried – gift cards, exclusive costume jewelry and, especially, the famous Christmas ornaments. It would be fun to work there, and she had always been greeted warmly. She even knew some of the clerks by name. Of course the badges they wore and the names embroidered on their aprons identified them. They were a nice group of women, even a few men, mostly close to her age. Then she saw the last few lines of the ad. *Must be able to work weekends, including Sunday.*

What? She shopped at the Hallmark store sometimes on Sundays, and she knew from things the women said both to customers and each other most of them were Christians. Still, she liked to reserve Sunday afternoons for her grandchild. Especially if there was a school choir event.

Patti loved her profession as a preschool

teacher at New Hope Christian school. She was one of the original teachers having started over fifteen years ago when New Hope first opened. She guessed she was the matriarch of the teachers. Miss Danica often deferred to her in meetings. It was both a compliment, and because she knew the school's history. She sighed and started to crumple the printed pages again.

Just before she tossed them back in the basket a small boxed ad caught her attention. Something about needing a Mrs. Santa Clause. Maybe because it was spelled wrong, and since she was a stickler for perfect English it had caught her eye. Having a degree in English Lit, although many years ago, hadn't been lost on her yet.

The ad stated interested candidates must appear in person Saturday at a local mall. It was a small mall, mostly with a grocery store, a shoe store and a few random shops. She remembered a music shop she had taken her granddaughter to for possible guitar lessons. No way would she let Tabitha take private lessons in a small closed room with a middle-aged, tattooed man. With thinning hair. Tabby, as everyone called her, was disappointed, to the tune of begging. She snickered at her own use of a pun. The child was adamant.

"Please, Grammy, please. He seems so nice, and his guitar is one of those special ones."

She'd finally calmed her down and explained while Tabby pouted.

Patti read the ad for Mrs. Santa again. It seems the business that was hiring sought someone authentic looking, both age wise and with a certain maturity. Working well with children was a plus, too, the ad said. That she could do.

TWO

Patti jockeyed her little car into the last handicap space. She was grateful her wonderful Dr. Kubitz, her pain doc, had given her one of those hanging things. He had offered a designated license plate, but sagely reminded her she could use the placard in any car she rode in. She tossed the plastic thing on her dashboard, stepped out and straightened her slacks.

Should she have worn a skirt? What did Mrs. Santa usually wear? Too late. Hiking up the waistband of her ridiculous red pants, the ones she only wore during Christmas season, and centering her feet in the Ugg boots, she fluffed out the Christmas sweater with Rudolph on the front. Another ridiculous piece of attire she'd bought because Tabitha had encouraged her last year.

"Grammy, you have to have this cute sweater to wear to that party. Look, you can even honk his nose."

Patti had worn the silly sweater to the preschool teachers' party and gotten a lot of laughs. She even won first prize for the silliest sweater. The

5

stash of candy canes was still in her pantry with the date not yet expired. Maybe she could bake something this holiday to use them in. Crushed, of course.

There was a line of about forty women in front of the grocery store. She was sure it wasn't Senior Day. That was always the first Wednesday each month, and this was the last Saturday in October. She stepped in line behind an overly abundant woman who wore too much perfume. Waving her hand in front of her, trying not to be obvious, she smiled when the woman turned around.

"Hi there! Guess we're here for the same gig," the large woman giggled. She reached out her hand toward Patti who shook its moist palm. "You ever done this before?"

Patti shook her head, but before she could answer the other woman spoke. "Been here every year. Never been chosen, but fun to try. Maybe today will be my lucky day."

Patti hoped the Mrs. Santa costume came in multiple sizes. *Nasty thought!* She touched the cross at her throat and prayed for forgiveness, and said thanks for her slim figure. Not that it would do much good as Mrs. Santa. Wasn't she plump?

The line moved more quickly than Patti had anticipated. The interviews must be only a few minutes each. Her heart sank. She had no chance. Oh, well, a silly fantasy. Maybe she should take the job at the gift store.

Suddenly it was her turn. "Next please. Step forward quickly." The man seated at the card table crumbled a paper and tossed it in a large waste basket beside him. He reached for the next paper in a pile beside him.

"Patricia Andrews, please step forward."

Three

Her heart pounded under the bulky sweater, and the Arizona heat didn't help. She felt dripping under her arms, and worse on her forehead. She must look a sweaty mess. So embarrassing. Briefly she wondered about the hefty woman in line ahead of her. Surely with her body weight she must have dripped, too. Poor thing. Patti said a brief prayer for her and wished she had asked her name.

"Ms. Andrews, please step forward." It was almost a growl. She envisioned her application being the next one crumbled and tossed. But she recalled the teen boy who had collected them from the women in line. He had glanced at her a bit longer than the women in front of her. "Good luck," he grinned. Maybe he'd said that to all the women and she just hadn't noticed.

She took a bigger step than planned, shuffled and caught herself just before lunging forward. Dang these heavy boots in the heat. Maybe it was the crumpled thick socks inside them that hindered her. "Yes, sir. Is there a problem?"

The middle-aged man with the perfect salved hair didn't even look at her for several moments.

When he did, she thought he resembled Simon Cowell. Strange. Couldn't be. Maybe this was really a tryout for the famous talent show.

"Turn around, please."

She did.

"Smile."

She did. Had she applied her lipstick straight?

"Bend toward me, please. I need to look at your hair."

That was weird, but he didn't touch her, just looked.

"Is this your natural color? No dyes, no artificial coloring?"

"Yes sir. No sir. Why?"

"Are you available during the Christmas holiday season from ten in the morning until seven every evening?"

Patti found herself nodding. But what about Sundays? She was too embarrassed to ask.

"I see on your application you are a preschool teacher. For how long?"

"Over fifteen years, sir. I helped to found the preschool. Teaching children is my blessing."

"Mmm. Whatever – as long as you know how to interact with little brats." He smirked. "And keep them in line."

"I'm sure I can control the children, if that's what you mean. But," she felt herself smirking back, "no children, no matter how unruly, are brats."

The smug man looked up at her, another smirk on his face. "How so?"

She straightened her shoulders prepared to set

this clueless man straight. "Sir, when children are acting like brats it usually means they are frightened or tired. Or both." She'd forgotten to add hungry. Oh, well. She wasn't sure he'd heard her, and if he had he would only shrug and say, "Whatever."

She had probably lost any opportunity for the job. Such a fun job hugging children and taking photos of them snuggled on Santa's lap. She didn't care. It was more important to enlighten this man. She wondered if he had children, and how they behaved.

~

"I thought I blew it!" she said to the reflection. "Guess not." One thing about mirrors is they can't talk back. One of the minor blessings of living alone. She ran her fingers through her hair and shook her head. That felt better. She wondered why that Simon Cowell look-alike was so interested in her scalp. Strange man.

Running her fingertips through her hair once more she talked to the mirror again. "Maybe it's time." The glass didn't voice its opinion. But Tabby had often voiced hers.

"Grams," she'd said. Patti hated when Tabby called her Grams. Grammy had been her chosen title when Jennifer was pregnant. Her friend Judy said this is the only time in your life when you get to chose your name. Chose well. She thought she had. But Tabby was an independent child, a free thinker for an eleven-year-old. Too bright sometimes in Patti's estimation. Still the child persisted.

"Grams?"

Patti was concentrating on her driving. They were on their way to Trader Joe's for Tabitha's favorite cookies. Usually Patti didn't indulge her grandchild in sugary sweets. But Tabby was a skinny little thing who actually ordered salads at Chick-fil-A. Without the cheese. She had recently won the art competition at her middle school. Her design was being put on all the school's choir's shirts. The girl deserved a treat.

"Yes, dear?" She bit her tongue to avoid saying, "Please don't call me Grams."

"Grams," she said again with determination, "isn't it time to dye your hair?"

Patti almost swerved to avoid another idiot Arizona driver. She said a silent prayer to thank Jesus for giving her control of her car and stellar quick reactions. She automatically threw her right arm across Tabitha's slender form. Just like her own mother had done years ago before seatbelts were invented.

"Whew! What were you saying, Tab?"

The child fiddled with the colored fingernails Patti had gifted her with. She had taken good care of them, all ten different colors. So fun, Patti had thought when she paid the bill.

"What, Tabby?"

"Uh, not so sure I should say this, but . . ." she grinned. "Gray hair makes you look old, Grammy."

So that was it. Gray equaled old. She had always been proud that her hair never looked yellow as some ladies' gray hair did. Like her friend Marsha's. But the woman was so sensitive Patti never brought it up.

She thought again about the Simon Cowell guy's interest in her hair. She guessed she had the job, but he never said why. Not exactly.

She'd grasped the papers he'd handed to her and spun on her Ugg boots back to her car. She'd barely opened the door with her shaking hands. Wiggling into the driver's seat and pulling down the sunscreen, she'd folded it to stuff between the two front seats. Finally, hands still shaking, she had pulled out of the grocery store lot and crept slowly up the parking aisle.

Maybe she should dye her hair.

Four

She opened the package, the one with the model in her twenties featuring long hair, that said *Try it. Temporary. Money back guarantee. Thirty days*. She laid out the stretchy gloves, the two little bottles, the plastic bowl for mixing and the directions. Oh, the shower cap. Got it all.

She called Tabitha. Yes, she was only eleven. But she was smart, and she had suggested this transformation.

"Tabby, I'm scared. Need help."

~

Tabitha stirred the concoction in the little blue bowl. Patti was sitting on a stool in front of the bathroom sink. How hard could this be?

"Uh, Grammy, this looks weird. See?" She held the tiny bowl up to Patti's nose. "Look. Smell."

"Yes. I bought the dark brown, the same hair color I used to have. What's wrong?"

"Not really you, first of all. But, smells strange, too."

"Why not really me? I want to be young again."

"Why? That's silly, Gram."

Patti bit her lip. There she goes calling me Gram again. "Stir, Tabby, stir. Start glopping it on."

She avoided reminding Tabitha it was her idea. Aw, to be eleven again. To voice opinions but not follow through.

Tabby tossed the brush down in the sink and put her hands on her hips. "Nope. Sorry. Can't do it."

"Why not? It's my hair, my choice." Patti heard the irritation in her voice and bit her lip again.

"It's just not you, Grammy. Besides," she wrinkled her brow, "aren't you going to be Mrs. Santa?"

"So?"

"I don't think Mrs. C. has brown hair. Didn't you say that man looked at your hair? And seemed to like its color?"

Why hadn't she thought of that? Maybe she'd been picked because of her whitish gray locks. But she could wear a wig. She mentioned this to Tabitha who shook her head adamantly.

"Too hot."

Five

Patti rinsed out the bowl and brush, shoved them back in the carton and put the whole mess in a trash bag. She wiped her eyes and blew her nose. Tabitha was right. The concoction smelled bad and made her nose run. Maybe she was allergic to it. What if she was and had applied it all over her head? Not worth the risk.

Tomorrow would be the teachers' Christmas luncheon, the final potluck party before the holiday break. Maybe, if she was brave enough, she would share about her holiday job, and get their opinions about her hair, too.

~

"What? You took a job? Not relaxing during Christmas break?"

"Are you crazy?"

"You bored?"

Patti made every effort to not physically put her hands on her ears. So much for support and confirmation. What, she wondered, did the other thirty-four teachers do. And the aides and the office staff. She loved to read, especially mysteries. She loved to bake and do crafts. She had even been trying to learn to knit and had signed Tabitha and her up for a Sunday afternoon lesson. The buzz words - crazy, bored - rang in her ears. She would not think them when she welcomed children and grandchildren into her arms as Mrs. Santa. Instead she would smile with enthusiasm, hopefully giving them assurance. And praying for them.

Tossing off the ridiculous Rudolph sweater with the honking nose she donned her favorite loose-fitting sweats and dialed the Simon Cowell man's phone. She was surprised that it was a local number. She'd expected a voicemail, even a corporate one.

"Hello." Oh goodness, he actually answered. Or was it a voicemail? Not sure, she frantically thumbed through the papers he'd given her. What was his actual name?

"Uh, Mr. Jefferson. Didn't really expect you to answer, was waiting for massage. A message," she corrected herself. He laughed.

"Glad you called Ms. Andrews."

"Oh. May I ask why?" She knew her voice was shaky, but sometimes it was when correcting three-year-old students. She waited for his answer and held her breath.

"First," his voice was firm. A good sign? Or was he going to terminate her before she even began?

"First," he continued, "I am impressed with your background, the long years as a teacher, especially of young children.

"Second," he paused, "are you still with me?"

She nodded then realized he couldn't see her.

"Yes, sir. Still here."

She decided to be brave. "How can I help you, sir?"

"First of all, call me Colin. So we can be friends. Okay?"

She sat down. What did he mean by that comment? She mentally skimmed through all the online advice about predators and how to be cautious and decided he was okay, genuine. Just an employer asking a favor of an employee. Was he that? Against her better judgment she answered.

Certainly, sir . . . uh, Colin. What can I do?"

"Help me with my grandson."

Six

Patti wrapped the red afghan around her body. How could she help this man? And his grandson? Not part of the job. Was God leading her to do it? Why had Colin and God led her there?

She threw off the afghan and stumbled to the bathroom. Splashing water on her face she looked in the vanity mirror again. She hadn't expected a response, but hoped for some kind of confirmation however simple. Did Jesus talk to her? Tell her what to do?

She noticed the cute sticker she'd put on the mirror, the one she'd also put on the mirror in the preschool teachers' bathroom. "Guess Who loves you." The answer below was Jesus.

The Colin guy really hadn't elaborated what the problem was with his grandchild. Nor, she realized, had she asked. She bumped a fist to her temple.

"Why did I just say sure and not ask for details?" The mirror didn't respond. Or did it by clouding up from her breath? She summoned up courage and texted him at the number he'd given her.

Mr. Colin. Want to talk about your grandson's

probs. Can we meet somewhere? It would have to be after church tomorrow around noon.

She felt pretty pleased with herself that Tabitha had taught her how to text. Now what?

Bing. Her cell. She pushed the button to open the message.

Can you meet me at Starbucks in the Safeway at FLW and Thompson Peak? I will be bringing Braydon, eleven.

Who was Braydon? The most difficult grandchild? Or his favorite?

Sure. Should I order hot chocolate for Braydon?

No response.

Why hadn't she asked about the child? Maybe she was losing her touch.

Seven

The service concluded with the usual invitation to "Give yourself to Jesus." Although, as requested, she didn't open her eyes to look around and see how many hands were raised. Up to the pastors to count, not her. She stuffed her phone and pretzel snack in her bag. This Sunday she would forego taking Communion. She didn't have time to sit and pray and thank, or think. Colin was probably waiting at the coffee shop. "Please, Jesus, you know I love to sup with You." She was sure He would understand. Hadn't He assigned this situation to her?

Colin sat at a round corner table twisting a paper cup. To Patti's trained eyes it must be a Venti. She skidded in next to him. "Double shot?"

"Decaf."

She nodded and clasped her hands in the folds of her skirt. Who was this troubled man, the one with the half-lidded eyes wiping them with a beige napkin?

"I thought you were bringing a grandson? Is he here?" She looked around and saw no children. Then she heard a shriek. And an announcement over the store's loudspeaker system.

"Would the parent of a child named Braydon please report to the Customer Service desk?"

"That's him. Gotta go. Sorry." Colin stood up with some difficulty. Maybe a knee or hip problem?

"I will come with you."

She reached for his hand. It was rough, and cold and dry. Pulling him forward was not an option. He stumbled, feet shifting. Finally he rose, and together they shuffled toward the front of the store, hand in hand.

They stood in line at the Customer Service Desk and locked eyes for a second. Why did Colin's look down? Embarrassed? She didn't have to ask. He offered.

"Braydon," he said, "is a troublesome child."

She couldn't resist asking. "Why?"

"Bad divorce. Custody battle."

"Oh. But, he's a good kid with problems?"

"Yep. But smart. In the top of his class. In advanced math. A super chess player. Won a lot of chess trophies."

"What an honor. Does anyone acknowledge that?"

"Sort of, sometimes."

"Who?"

"His mom, my daughter, does. But it's hard. She has three other kids." Colin wiped his brow with another beige napkin. "All girls," he added.

"What about others?" She didn't want to ask about the other parent, so she bit her tongue. Still, she blabbed on. "Sounds like he needs a strong father figure." Colin nodded. "You up to that?" she asked. Where had that invasive comment come from? So bold and inappropriate. But Colin nodded and squeezed her hand.

They walked toward the Customer Service Desk and stood in line behind three people buying lotto tickets. She held her tongue. Why would people waste money? Colin pulled out his wallet. What? He was going to buy a ticket?

"No, no, no, Colin. No!"

He looked at her in confusion and shook his head.

"Uh, I was just getting my drivers license out to prove I'm Braydon's grandpa."

"Oh. Sorry."

Eight

"Braydon!" Colin spread his arms wide. No one entered. He looked confused, then his face blotched red.

"What did you do?"

A slim child with unruly blonde hair shuffled his feet.

Patti offered her hand. "Hi, Braydon. My name is Patti. I'm your grandpa's friend."

When the child didn't respond she hunkered down. Ugh, tough on her knees. She noticed a nearby lawn chair on sale next to the self-service checkout section and dragged it over.

Finally sitting, she leaned forward and grabbed his hands in hers. Was that appropriate? She wasn't sure, but it came naturally. The hands were limp, so she clasped harder.

"Braydon, I'm a teacher. I want to help you. What's wrong?"

The last clasp of her hands must have done it. Or did God? He lowered his face to hers.

"I wanted chips," he said in a shaky voice. "Just wanted chips. Grandpa said I could have them."

Patti looked at the tear-filled eyes and made a decision she hoped she wouldn't regret, or lose her new job for.

Colin started to speak, but she waved her hand to silence him as she noticed the grimace on his rugged face.

"So, Braydon, what exactly did your grandpa say?"

More shuffling feet, another lowered face. "I would have to behave and talk with the nice lady meeting us. Guess I didn't do that."

"Mmm. Guess not. Why not?"

Suddenly the boy looked straight at her. "Are you the nice lady?"

"I sure hope so."

"Are you and Grandpa friends?"

"I hope so."

"Do you go to church?"

Patti was taken back by the boy's question. Where did that come from?

"Yes, every Sunday. Sometimes on Wednesdays. Why do you ask?"

Braydon lowered his head and shrugged. "Don't know. Curious."

"But you must have a reason for asking, Braydon."

Another shrug.

Colin and Patti each took a hand and led the boy back to the table in the Starbucks sitting area. He didn't resist or pull away. A good sign?

"Would you like some hot chocolate, Braydon?" When Colin shook his head no, she kicked him under the table.

"Sorry." She grinned but had no remorse. Getting the child to open up was more important than warm chocolate.

"Whipped cream? Extra sprinkles." She had to nudge Colin's leg again. What was wrong with the man?

"Yeah, sure." The boy fiddled with the crumpled napkin she and Colin had left on the table. Then he raised his face to look at her.

"Why are you being so nice to me?"

"Uh, just what I do, Braydon. You okay with it?"

"Sort of, I guess. The only woman who is usually nice to me is my mom, and one teacher."

"Really? How sad. What is that special teacher like? What is her name?" Patti worried she was going too far, so she said her silent prayer. The one Jabez said about enlarging his borders.

"Mrs. Aaronson. But, she's Jewish. So Grandpa says she doesn't count."

Patti felt anger reaching up through her bones. What had Colin said to this child? Because a teacher wasn't Christian she didn't count? Did the man ever read a Bible? Did he know God put all kinds of people in our paths to love and encourage us, sometimes even non-believers. Often non-believers.

Nine

Wiping off her makeup somehow brought her closer to God. Silly observation. Clean skin, just the way God made her. She tossed the tissue in the trash under the sink and thought back to today. What was that child telling her? Why did Colin react as he had? Maybe with sleep the answer would come.

She and Colin had calmed the boy, and Colin had walked him to his car with a hot chocolate overflowing with whipped cream, plus lots of abundant sprinkles. Patti's mouth had salivated, still did. If only there weren't so many calories.

She thought about the child. She knew about divorce situations from her long experience as a teacher. Every day she encountered children coping with the loss of a two-parent household. So many times, too often, the kids blamed themselves. So sad. So super sad.

Sometimes a small change could bring relief, if only temporary relief. Sometimes it could help. A week later the call came.

~

Normally, no random calls came on a Sunday

morning. But the number was local. Still she hesitated. When a nasty female voice started to scream horrible words and, "Who are you to upset my son?" she was sorry she'd picked up. Probably shouldn't have. Too late.

Patti didn't respond. But her hands were shaking and her knees were unsteady. She was sure who the woman was, although she didn't know her name. She needed to call Colin. She reminded herself it was Sunday morning. Maybe she would see him in church. Hopefully.

The church was packed. One of those Sundays when an almost famous guest pastor was speaking. She loved Pastor Terry and his son Pastor Tylor, but the other visiting speakers were always phenomenal. Usually.

Today she couldn't absorb the message about David and his "incident" with Bathsheba. Instead she felt as if she was up against a Goliath. What had Pastor Terry said last week when he had delivered his message? Something about lessons in the Bible, even difficult lessons. Oh, yes, David was a man after God's own heart. Even with all his sins and mistakes, God loved and honored him. God was always protecting his back.

She knew it wasn't the same, even felt remorse and guilt that she would compare. But she needed God to protect her back and give her the confidence David had when confronting Goliath. She had a good relationship, now friendship, with Colin. But the woman on the phone? Was she Patti's Goliath? Or was Braydon?

~

27

Patti stood in line at the omelet station. She was treating herself to one at AJ's Market patio so she could eat outside, alone. Rick, the omelet chef according to his name tag, shook his head and his small ponytail tossed. He was preparing and flipping three omelets. Such a gift. She always had trouble making one small one for herself without ruining it. Finally hers, the third one, was slathered with shredded cheddar cheese. She reached to accept it and laughed.

"Rick, why the Santa hat? It's still November."

"I love Christmas," he said with a wide grin. "I feel in the spirit."

"Hi, Santa!"

The voice behind her sounded familiar. Too familiar.

"I want a Santa waffle special."

She leaned toward the child and offered a high five. He looked at her curiously, then started to shuffle away. Why did this child shuffle? Most pre-teen boys sauntered in their attempt to look more grown up.

"Wait, Braydon! I just wanted to say hi and happy Sunday."

His back was still turned toward her when she heard another familiar voice.

"Braydon, don't be rude. Say hello to Miss Patti." Colin looked apologetically at her.

"It's okay, Colin. Maybe he's feeling shy today."

"Shouldn't be. Had a great message in church about David. Braydon's middle name, ya know."

She hadn't. She didn't know the relevance, but

she smiled and was more concerned about Colin's attitude than Braydon's. What was going on? Had the two of them been in her church?

Ten

Black Friday!

Why would the Santa days start on it? She used to love shopping with Jennifer, then later when Tabitha had grown old enough to be out late at night with them. How fun it was to stand in line at Target to chat with others and be one of the next fifteen to be let into the store. Now it was pure bedlam. No lines, no numbered tickets, just chaos and confusion. The thrill of adventure was gone.

She struggled into the Mrs. Santa attire and pulled on her Ugg boots. Colin had casually said she could wear them because they looked authentic. Was anything about this day real?

Fluffing her hair with a bit of hairspray and shoving the Christmas Tree earrings into the allotted ear holes, she checked herself in the mirror for the tenth time.

"I look ridiculous," she said to the image. Again it didn't respond. She shouldered her hefty purse and skipped to her car. Maybe skipping would put her in the right mood.

Her first assignment was the local market.

Seemed strange to have a Santa there, but she wasn't the one who decided. She secured her purse behind the bearded man's chair, picked up the instant camera to be ready for photo ops. The thing that confused her was how to take the money parents paid for the photos. When Jennifer and her brothers were little no cost was involved. Only wiggling and crying and a patient Santa and stressed parents. Now parents had to pay for the precious photo that would go into the album or on the Christmas card.

She looked for a bucket or bowl for "cash donations," as they were diplomatically called. There were neither. Instead a strange device was thrust into her hand by the frowning Santa.

"Just hold it out. Have them slide a card in it. When it beeps it's done and prints out a receipt. Hand that to them. That's all. Super simple."

Okay. She set the small black device at her feet. She could pick it up when needed. Right?

The first customers were a group of four. She mentally checked her English grammar. Was it "was" a group or "were" it a group? Giving up she tried to settle the four children in Santa's lap. He was a big man, but his lap couldn't accommodate all four. The mother insisted.

"How about the two little ones each sit on a knee, and the older ones snuggle up to Santa's shoulders? That would look so cute." Fortunately, the older girls gave Santa a kiss on each cheek, so the mother was pleased, and at least placated. She had swiped her credit card, faked a smile and walked off. Whew! That wasn't too hard.

The next one was easy. One child who was excited to tell Santa his list. Santa was barely accommodating with a smile, a "Ho, ho," and a grin. Happy child, happy mom. Yay!

The day went on without much incident. She and Santa had a brief lunch in the supermarket's break room. She hadn't counted on the long flight of stairs to get to it, but convinced herself it was good for her heart and legs. It had been fun chatting with the young men and women who were assigned to bag groceries at the end of each checkout line. Most were mentally challenged, and some hooted strange noises. They all had a monitor person who looked after them while working and who made sure they didn't behave inappropriately in gesture or speech. She admired that person. What a job.

After several hours it was almost time to close shop. Her feet were hot in the boots, and she was sure Santa was warm in his attire. She smiled at the strange man. He hadn't been super jolly as she'd expected. Not happy in his job? He'd not taken off his costume during their brown bag lunch. Just shoved food in his mouth and guzzled a Diet Pepsi. No conversation, even though she'd tried. Just nods and guttural sounds. She had given up.

Now it was almost closing time. No children were lined up, so she took a risk.

"So, never caught your name, Santa."

She was awarded with a scowl. "Nope. Yours neither."

"Since we will be working together for a while, it might be nice to be more friendly."

Another scowl, and a grunt.

Suddenly she felt bold. "What's your problem, buddy? This is supposed to be a fun gig."

"I don't like children, kids, brats. You got that?"

Eleven

Patti splashed warm water on her face to remove the rosy cheeks and dark brows. She didn't understand those, since she was supposed to be Mrs. Claus with almost white hair she'd powdered to make her gray hair appear whiter. Why hadn't she been instructed to dye or change her black brows? Didn't make sense. Maybe to define her eyes? A lot didn't make sense, including why that grumpy man was playing Santa.

Glaring in the mirror to remove the last remnants of her brown brows, she had an idea. No. Not appropriate. Or was it?

The day had been okay, but boring and not fun. Not even the parents were excited. Another element was needed to add joy. It was only eight o'clock, not too late. No school tomorrow for Winter Break, as it was diplomatically called, instead of what it really is, Christmas Break.

She dialed.

~

"I'm so excited, Grams. Mom says it's a go and I can dress in my Christmas plaid skirt."

Patti bit her tongue. What was the thing Tabby

had about calling her "Grams?" What was wrong with "Grammy" the name she'd chosen? Oh, well, at least the exuberant child would stand by her and look adorable. If she could get approval from Colin. She learned the next morning that would be the biggest hurdle.

When she showed up for work she was surprised to see Colin there. What a stroke of luck. He was probably checking the situation since both she and the Rent-a-Santa were part of his company. She introduced him to Tabitha who smiled brightly and almost curtsied as she extended her hand.

"She can't be here! She's a child. We could be accused of child labor. Even arrested."

When the smoke finally stopped coming out of his ears, Patti placed her hands on his shoulders. Such a familiar gesture, but since the Braydon incident she thought it was okay.

"Calm down, Colin. She is not working. She will not be paid. *Except by me in Justice for Girls dollars*, she whispered under her breath. Tabby loved the cute clothes at that store, and Patti had so much fun taking her. Pressing on, she drew herself up to full Mrs. Santa height. Today her brows were white. After removing the makeup last evening she decided to check the instructions for her job. Pulling the printed paper from under her cosmetic basket she gasped.

"All facial hair must appear white. All extremities, arms and legs, even chest, must either be covered or be whitened. Covered is preferred. Skirts should be below the knees, hands clothed in gloves, feet in boots appropriate for winter. You are to look like Mrs. Santa as much as possible."

Oh. Ah. Now she understood. Even her four-year-old preschool students would have gotten it. Why hadn't she? Nerves, or the budding friendship with Grandpa Colin?

"Colin, she is not working. At least not for you. She is my sidekick. She can even pretend to be an elf sitting at grumpy Santa's feet," she quipped.

"He's grumpy?"

"Yep. Man has no personality. At least none that attracts kids." There, she's said it. She was sorry, but she had no idea who Grumpy was. Just that he was, well, grumpy.

Colin stomped off waving his hands in the air. She decided Tabby could stay, but gave her strict instructions to be low-keyed.

"What does that mean, Grammy?"

Patti almost threw kisses to heaven. The child actually called her "Grammy."

"It means," she said with as much authority as she could muster, "you are to be my sidekick. Don't do or say anything unless I prompt you."

"Does that mean you will tell me?"

"Maybe. Maybe not. I might tap you on the shoulder. Just use your best judgment, please. And don't do anything over the top. Okay?"

"Got it, Grammy."

Maybe Jennifer had drilled it in to her to call her grandmother by the name she'd chosen. The girl looked so cute in the elf sweater Patti had splurged on at Justice for Girls last year. She was glad it still fit her and grateful she'd had that coupon.

Twelve

People were lined up to see Santa when Patti and Tabby arrived at the Santa throne. They were already in their costumes so they only had to sidle near the bearded man.

Tabby pulled on Patti's arm lowering her grandma's ear to whisper. "Why is he so grumpy? He's not a jolly Santa, Grams."

Patti ignored the remark and squeezed Tabby's hand. "Let's pray for him."

Santa squeezed himself into his throne. Tabby suppressed a giggle. Did she also think it was overdone, too opulent, too much gold? Or did she think, as Patti did, that the Santa man wasn't a good fit, both personality wise and physically? She reminded herself again she was not in charge. In a few days she would get a paycheck. Maybe then she would quit. If she did, who would take her place as Mrs. Santa? The over weight woman in line in front of her who had tried for years? What a blessing that would be for her.

~

The music started to play *Here Comes Santa Claus*. How appropriate. Two children came forward. A woman hesitated with a camera clutched to her chest and looked around nervously. Almost as if she was afraid. Was there fear in her eyes? Patti wasn't sure if this was one of the security situations she'd been cautioned to look for. No one had given specifics, just statements saying to be wary. And push the button if concerned.

Patti looked down at the little black thing to slide credit cards into. Was there a button on it? Where? She started to pull Tabby close to her when Tabby broke loose and approached the woman. Almost grabbing the woman's camera, she said, "May I? I'd love to take your picture with the children."

The woman offered the camera to Tabby, wiped her eyes and wrapped her arms around the two children. All three were snuggled next to a suddenly smiling Santa when the camera clicked.

Then Security showed up.

~

Tabitha was shaking under the wing of Patti's arm. Patti kept rubbing Tab's shoulder and whispering what she thought were calming words, mostly "Shh, shh" into the girl's ear.

"Wha . . . what happened, Grammy? Why was that woman arrested?"

Patti wished she knew. How could she explain to an eleven-year-old? Finally she said the truth. "I don't know, can't even guess."

Two Security persons suddenly pulled her aside and behind a cloistered area near the women's restroom. "Leave the girl," the male one said.

"NO! She is my granddaughter. I will never

leave her."

The female officer smiled and gave the male officer a look that put him in his place. At least that was Patti's interpretation.

"I do need to ask you both some questions. That okay, Grandma?"

Before Patti could nod, a small, but strong, voice said, "I want to know what's happening. I was there."

"Maybe, Tabby, you should wait until the officer asks."

"No, Ma'am, it's okay. If you are okay with me asking the young lady some questions."

"I'm ready." Tabitha pulled herself up to her full four-foot ten height.

After Tabby explained how she had grabbed the camera from the woman to take the special photo, and had given it back, she still had questions.

"That was very brave of you, Tabitha. But you probably shouldn't have done it. Not in the job description." Ms. With A Too Long Name to Remember, smiled. "Still, I am proud of you for caring about those children."

"I just wanted to make the mom happy. And, I still want to know why she was arrested."

~

Patti made hot chocolate and snuggled Tabby on the sofa with one of the old dog blankies. Probably the one Sam the bigger shedder had used. Oh, well, Jennifer had a washer.

"Grammy?" The question hung in the air. At least the child used her special name.

"Yes?"

"Why was that mother arrested? I thought I was doing something nice for her. She didn't look like she even knew how to take a good picture. I wanted it to be special for her, for her memory book."

Should she explain? Patti was conflicted, but Tabby was a smart kid.

"That mother, Tab, did not have custody of those children."

"Why not? Don't mothers usually get the kids?"

"I guess not in this case." Patti chose her words carefully, but Tabitha deserved to know.

"According to the woman officer the mother took the kids and brought them to see Santa when they were staying with a caregiver who didn't know the rules. I suppose she desperately wanted a loving picture with her children. But she wasn't supposed to . . . legally."

"Why not? What was wrong with her that she can't have her own kids?"

"It was a court decision, a judge's decision. I don't know." But she wished she did.

Patti asked Jennifer, Tabby's mother, if the girl could stay the night. She tucked her in to the second side of her queen bed. The blankie that used to be Sam the Shredder's landed at her feet. Oh, well, Tabby had loved the dogs. Maybe time to think about adopting again. Living alone can be so lonely.

After Tabby fell asleep, when Patti detected quiet snoring, she decided to call Colin. His answer was disturbing.

BONNIE ENGSTROM

Thirteen

"What do you want?"

"Uh, never mind. Sorry. Another time." She hung up. She wished she had called him on her landline so she could bang the receiver. He had said to call him any time. Apparently, this was not one of those.

He called back. Should she answer? Why not?

"Sorry, Patti. Stressful day. I heard what happened at the Santa viewing today. You okay?"

"I'm okay. My granddaughter is a little undone, though. I thought your company that runs this Santa thing should be in the loop."

"You mean Santa Extravaganza? That's me. Alone."

"Oh."

"I guess you assumed it was some big company? Maybe international, or at least statewide? Well, it's not." He paused during Patti's silence. "It does explain it on the paperwork I gave you. Yes, it's bonafide, and before you ask, we are highly insured. For everything possible," he added.

"Everything?"

"Well, almost." The breath he blew out was

more than a sigh.

"What about the situation today? A mother illegally taking, maybe abducting, her children? Then being caught with Santa?" Her turn to blow out a long breath. "I know you aren't responsible for that, but it's bound to be in the papers and on the news. Could hurt," she blew out another breath, "the image of visiting Santa. Not only yours, but other Santas. Maybe," she said, "even Christmas."

"I'm trying to process that." Finally he asked about Tabitha. "How is your granddaughter. Was she traumatized?"

"She's okay. When we got home I made hot chocolate and she snuggled on my sofa under a dog blanket. When she fell asleep I tucked her into bed."

"How do you do that? Calming her, I mean?"

Patti wasn't sure how to answer. Maybe it was a grandma thing, or a teacher thing or a faith thing.

"I just do it. Comes naturally with the territory."

She regretted her response. After all she was a woman, a mother and grandmother, and a teacher. The response to Colin was a bundle of all those. What was that saying about men being clueless? Not their fault since Eve took the first bite. But, still, hadn't they learned anything in two thousand years?

~

Fortunately, the incident of the mother wanting to take a photo of her kids with Santa did not appear in the paper or online. Patti hoped that it was Divine Intervention that avoided it.

Since it was Winter Break for all local schools,

they decided to meet in the sitting area near Starbucks in Safeway again. This time they would each bring a grandchild. Tabitha was thrilled with the idea.

"Do I get to tell my story, Grammy? About the woman and Santa and the kids?"

Patti shuffled her feet. Should she shush Tabby or let her blab? After all, it was her story since she had grabbed the camera from the woman, then took the photo.

"I guess, but only if Mr. Jefferson asks."

"Okay."

Patti noticed Tabby was shifting on her feet and wiggling. Not her usual confident behavior. Probably excited about meeting the man who set up the Santa situations. Is that what they are? Situations?

Suddenly Tabby pulled from her grasp and ran forward. She stood as tall as her four-foot- eight height allowed and planted herself in front of Colin with her arms at her sides and her hands in fists. What was the child doing?

Colin stopped in his tracks; feet locked in place. He looked over Tabby's head to connect his eyes with Patti's. The confusion on his face said more than she wanted to infer. She lowered her lids and smiled, hoping that would do. Coward.

Tabby extended her hand, actually almost threw it at the confused man. He looked at it blankly. After Tabby's hand quivered a few times, he got it. Pulling his large hand from the pocket on his jacket, he lifted it toward her.

"Hello again Miss Tabitha." It was almost a

question, but he was rewarded with a grin. He gripped her small hand in both of his and knelt down to her eye level. "Thank you for coming to visit with me."

Patti could only think of the old expression "blown away." Where was the Colin she knew, the staunch businessman and the almost bitter grandpa?

After ordering the morose looking extra pump decaf latte for Colin, the fat-free tea with no sugar for Patti, and finally the trente strawberry acai refresher with lemonade, 3 scoops of strawberry and 3 scoops of dragon fruit, all blended, for Tabitha they settled around a corner table.

"Where's Braydon?" Tabitha burst out as usual. No filter.

"Uh, didn't want to come."

"Why not?"

"Not sure."

"Aren't children supposed to do what grandparents ask?"

"Tabby, you are being too forward. If Braydon didn't want to come that's not your business."

"I don't mind explaining, Patti. Or Tabitha," he tilted his head in her direction.

"Braydon is having some difficulties."

Before Colin could finish speaking, Tabitha blurted out. "What kind?"

"Hard to explain, Tabby. May I call you that?"

"Sure, I guess. My family is the only one who does. But I guess you're special," she added. "Like almost family."

Colin covered his mouth with both hands and turned away coughing racking sounds.

46

"You okay?" Tabitha burst out. "You sick?"

"No, no. Must be the weather, the sudden moisture in the air. Always gets me."

"Okay. So, what's Braydon's problem?" Tabby looked the man full in the face. "Come clean."

"Tabby!" Patti was adamant and embarrassed. "How rude!"

"Grammy, you always told me to be honest."

"Well . . ." she hesitated, "not that honest."

"Sorry. Just want to help."

Colin was covering his mouth again to suppress more choking laughter. He turned back to high five Tabitha. "You are one interesting girl, Tabby," he managed to say until he continued with his laughing spate.

Tabby grinned. "Thanks, Mr. J."

Patti wanted to disappear and fade into the wall decorated with the strange wallpaper behind the round tables. Instead she summoned her best grandma stance and yanked Tabitha away.

Pulling the girl into the market's deli section and cloistering behind the chicken wings bar, she hoped she was being very stern.

"Tabby, I am embarrassed. Your behavior is even beyond you. What were you thinking to speak to Mr. Jefferson that way?"

"Grammy," she said putting her hands on her narrow hips, "I was being honest. Didn't you always tell me to be? And," she continued, "you said two things. One, Braydon would be here so I could meet him. Two, Mr. Anderson is having trouble being a grandpa. Just being honest and doing what you asked."

Patti shook her head. Tabby was right, but she was too right. At eleven she should have been more discreet. The girl really did have no filter.

"Still, Tab, not your place to question a grownup. You were impertinent. Know what that means?" She was sure Tabby did with all her English language skills. Still, worth asking.

"Uh, disrespectful? Rude? Impolite?"

Patti nodded. "You must stop this. Now. Understand? And, you must apologize to Mr. Anderson. Right now!"

Fourteen

Patti dipped her toe in the hot bubbly water. A soak would feel so good. Bubble baths were always her favorite. She tossed another bath bomb underneath the faucet for good measure and sunk into the foaming bliss.

Her sigh was interrupted by the bing of her phone. Someday she needed to look up Murphy's Law on Google. Thanks, or maybe not, to the new feature on her phone she heard the voicemail message. What did he mean, "Let's meet at church?" She didn't even know he went to church. Then she remembered he mentioned hearing the story of David last Sunday. Must be the same church she went to. Mmm.

~

She didn't usually go to the Wednesday night service. But he had requested.

She hesitated down one of the several aisles. He didn't say where he would be sitting. Or even if he was coming. When she called him back he didn't answer. So why was she here?

She felt a touch on her elbow and turned.

"Hi, Mr. Mysterious. Didn't know you

attended."

"Just once in a while." He grinned that lop-sided one she had come to cherish, even in her dreams. What was she thinking? She didn't even know if he was single. Surely God wouldn't have given her those dreams if Colin was not available.

"So, what makes this 'once in a while' the right one?" She hoped her own lopsided grin would encourage him to share.

"An opportunity to see you. Couldn't think of another way." There was that grin again.

The service began, and she raised her hands during the praise songs. It gave her such freedom to lift them up to the Lord. Colin was standing rigid next to her. Should she hold back? Instead she turned to him and hugged him during the 'greet your neighbor' sixty seconds Pastor Lisa encouraged. Had she shocked him instead of just shaking his hand? Where was Tabby to give her sage advice?

Colin looked at her with confusion. She waved her hand in front of her face and said, "Sorry. Didn't mean to embarrass."

"No, no. It was so nice to hug you. Finally."

~

Patti plunked her purse on the booth bench and spread her skirt. She loved IHop, but it wasn't her favorite go-to dinner place. Sometimes she took Tabby here for the pancake blitz, but never for the real dinner menu. Usually breakfast. Still, she was grateful to be sitting opposite Colin. Maybe she could learn more. She scanned the Fifty-five Plus dinner menu. Ugh. Grilled chicken, tilapia, roast turkey. That was for Thanksgiving. She wasn't in the mood for fish, and turkey was only for Thanksgiving. She scanned the other options and made a choice.

Craving a giant hamburger she told the server, "I want a Mega Monster burger. With extra cheese and avocado. Fries on the side, please. Lots of ranch dressing for the fries."

"Wow! You are a woman who loves to eat!"

Was that a compliment or a disapproval?

"It's only a few dollars more than the senior menu options. I will pay."

Colin's face drained of all color. "So sorry, Patti, I meant that in jest. No problem paying for anything you want. I hope you will order dessert."

She reached her hand across the table to touch his fingers. "I'm sorry, too. Just over-reacted. Not used to having a man pay for my dinner." She saw the relief on his face, squeezed his fingers and grinned. "Been alone too long I guess."

Colin squeezed back and nodded. "You lonely, too?"

Fifteen

Once more the bubble bath seemed perfect for thinking. She dipped her toe in and sank into oblivion. This time she had turned off her phone. No interruptions. She hoped for solace. Peace and bubbles.

Exactly what had Colin said? Or at least inferred? Yes, she was lonely, but she had Jennifer and Tabitha and all the co-workers and teachers. She managed to fill her time. God had gifted her with special people in her life. Patti slipped under the bubbles and blew them out with pursed lips. Toweling off with her favorite white terrycloth, she thought back to their conversation over dinner. She donned the robe from her one extravagant visit to a Marriott Hotel and pushed the buttons on her phone.

Without any preamble she blurted out, "What did you mean asking me if I was lonely, too?"

"Hi, Miss Patti. This is Braydon. I'm answering Grandpa's phone for him."

"Uh, Hi, Braydon." Silence. Breathing. "You still there? Where is your grandpa?"

"I'm not supposed to tell anyone because it's not man-like. But," the young voice suddenly had a prepubescent whispery squeak, "he's taking a bubble bath." Another silence. "He says Winston Churchill took them, too. And," he added, "he was an important man."

Patti tried to control her mirth, then gave up. Holding her stomach she collapsed on the padded bench in her bedroom. Laughter spurted forth like a geyser. She heard voices coming from her phone but they were too distant to distinguish words, just the tone of the words. Shouting? Who was shouting, and who was crying? She guessed but didn't want to pursue the conversation. If one could call it that. Finally, she hung up. Still holding her tummy, she slipped into a pair of silk pajamas, combed her hair and brushed her teeth. To be sure of no interruptions she double pushed the little bar on the side of her phone to red to silence it and ignored the intermittent buzzing. Probably served Colin right for allowing an eleven-year-old to answer. She turned out the light, clicked the TV remote and snuggled under the covers. The last thing she remembered hearing was the loud pre-set silence of the television turning off. Winston Churchill indeed!

She awoke to her own snoring and sunlight seeping through the sliding door shutters. And the buzzing sound her phone makes when she had it on hushed mode. The sounds were intermittent, so she figured some were calls and some were texts. That man! She was sure he was embarrassed that Braydon told her about his secret bubble bath. She reset her phone and answered the latest call.

~

"I hope you didn't punish the boy. He's only eleven and was being honest, as I also hoped you had taught him to be."

"Ma'am? Are you all right?"

"Uh. Who is this?"

"This is Steve from Cox Communications, Ma'am. Just confirming our appointment for this morning."

"Oh. Sorry. I forgot."

"This is Patti Tutor, isn't it?"

She nodded and realized the confused person on the other end couldn't hear her head rattle. "Yes, this is she. What time did you say you're coming? Nine is fine. Thank you."

She snickered at her deception. When she'd first moved in, alone, she decided to not give her real surname to public companies. She had to give it to the electric company and the gas company with her Social Security number to verify who she was. But the communications company, the landscapers and the cleaners who picked up her laundry didn't need it. Just a pin for each. She had chosen a fictitious substitute word of teacher. She had thought it very clever. What was that called? Onomatopoeia? No. Malapropism? No. Euphemism? So frustrating since she prided herself on her English expertise. Maybe she was getting old. *Well, let's just call it like it is, a way to protect a single woman without giving away her personal information. That'll do.*

She had just donned her gray sweats when the doorbell rang. Frustrated she hadn't had time for makeup she had at least brushed her hair. She doubted the communication technician would care. He probably saw a lot of older women without makeup. Still, before she went to the door she spritzed herself with Este Lauder Intense, her favorite cologne. She liked to smell nice, even for repair people.

She put on her best smile and pulled back the big wood door. "Hi! So glad you came. Really need your help."

"Me, too!" Colin leaned forward, a huge grin on his face. Braydon stood next to him teary eyed.

"Oh, my! You aren't the computer repair man."

"Nope. Coming in."

"Sure. Why not?" She regretted that stupid comment immediately. Too late to take it back.

"I am surprised. That's all." Would that redeem her socially with her boss?

Colin marched right in and settled himself in her big "read chair." That's what Tabby called the red chair, "the read chair" where Patti often read before bed.

Braydon stood statue-like with his eyes cast on the Oriental carpet.

"Comfy?" She glared at Colin. Now she was being sarcastic.

"Yes. Nice chair, good cushions. Almost as good as a bubble bath," he snickered.

"Okay, Colin, what's up with the impromptu visit?" She knew she still didn't sound very welcoming, but he had burst into her home without an invitation. Not even a warning. Cad.

"Braydon David here," he gestured into the air in her living room, as if Braydon wasn't standing right in front of him, "has something to say. Don't you Bray?"

The child shuffled his feet, clasped his hands behind him and scowled at his grandfather.

"Wipe that look off your face and do what you came here to do. Now."

Sixteen

Patti brushed her teeth for the third time hoping to get the bad taste out of her mouth and her heart. What was going on? She tried to process and remember the situation. Poor Braydon. So embarrassed, so coerced to make an apology. She hoped she'd been gracious and loving to the child, even apologizing herself. Although she wasn't sure what for. No matter. The boy was obviously uncomfortable and Colin had forced him to come. Who was Colin? Not the man she thought and hoped for. She needed to find out and take action. Mr. Santa or not!

She dialed.

~

"What in heavens name were you thinking? That was no way to show love to a grandchild."

When she heard no response she hung up. The man was now on the top of her list. What list she wasn't sure. She no longer cared about him, but she was very concerned about his grandparenting skills, and Braydon.

She was due to don her Mrs. Santa outfit and "Ho, Ho," and smile, and take pictures in an hour.

Glancing in the mirror she realized she had never put on makeup. Not even her regular daily makeup, plus the elaborated version for her Mrs. Santa role. She applied it more carefully than usual, selfishly hoping the children would be enticed to approach her before that old curmudgeon with the fake beard. She pinched her cheeks to make them look rosier than the Paris Red rouge. Laughing at the name of the product she swiped its companion lipstick across her mouth. Adjusting the silly cap, bonnet, or whatever it was called, she thumbed her nose in the mirror. She would "one up" Colin and . . . what?

She wanted to beat herself up for not defending Braydon. Colin had been so adamant about making the child apologize to her. For what? She wasn't sure if it was because the boy had shared the secret of his grandpa taking a bubble bath, or? She couldn't remember anything rude or offensive the child had said. He had courteously called her by name, Miss Patti, as she had been introduced to him. He was a delightful child, other than the time they had to rescue him in Safeway. Or had they rescued Safeway from him? Still he had been courteous then, almost remorseful, apologizing to the woman behind the Customer Service Counter.

The incessant ting-a-linging from her phone interrupted her thoughts. She really should try to change the ring tone. She had promised herself to go to the local Verizon store for assistance, but time and schedules always got in the way. She had expected Colin to call and apologize.

Thank goodness he did right before their Mr. and Mrs. Santa gig. She tried to hold her anger in check, but it burst forth.

"It's about time you called." She knew she was shouting, but frankly at this point didn't care. "You have no business caring for a grandchild, even having one. I will see you in an hour, even though I'd rather work for another Santa."

The silence on the other end infuriated her more. At least the man could respond and defend himself. The cad.

"Couldn't you at least say something?"

"Uh, yes ma'am. Are you okay?"

"Who are you? Is this Braydon again answering for your grandpa?"

"No, ma'am. My name is Richard. From the TV repair company." The voice paused. "Are you still there, Ma'am?"

Oh glory be! She'd done it again.

Seventeen

She tugged on her boots at the last minute. She preferred her Ugg boots, more comfortable, but the new written job description insisted she wear the green vinyl ones. Too hot. Plastic. Did Mrs. Santa wear plastic in the North Pole? Amelia, the young woman whose title was "dresser" laughed and helped her pull on the boots. "Maybe she does now in the twenty-first century," she giggled. Smart girl, Amelia. Will probably go places.

She hadn't brought Tabitha today. Too much stress going on between her and Colin. Tabby would surely pick up on that and ask some intimidating questions.

After wiggling into the boots she adjusted her skirt and took her place next to Santa. Why did he look different and his "Ho, Ho" sound different? Deeper, more baritone. She was no vocal expert, but she remembered Colin's voice from his "Ho, Ho, Hos" that time he took over for the annoying, gruff Santa after the sad situation with the mother who wanted a picture with her kids. Maybe he had a cold? If he did, he shouldn't be snuggling young children on his knees. His cheeks were redder, too.

Maybe he did have a cold. Not her concern, though.

The first child who approached was about five. Confirmed when Santa asked him. She chuckled that being a Kindergarten teacher gave her an edge guessing ages. Oh, my gosh, he was one of her students. She lowered her chin and turned away slightly hoping Darrin didn't recognize her. He wouldn't have until his overbearing mother screamed.

"Darrin, look who's here! Your teacher." The woman tugged on the boy's sleeve and practically dragged him to Patti. She debated. Should she try to remain incognito or admit the deception? Truth was important to Patti, so truth won out.

She opened her arms for a hug feeling blessed that teachers in Christian schools could hug students without reservation. Darrin grinned widely and ran into them. He had just gotten, "So cool, Miss Patti" out of his mouth when she felt a hand gripping her elbow.

"Security, Ma'am. Come with me," the bulky officer in the blue uniform announced.

She was led around the curtain and frisked. Was that really necessary?

"What is going on? I did nothing wrong."

"You hugged a child. Against regulations. In the contract." The officer looked contrite, but his voice was deep and threatening.

"But, I'm a teacher, and he is one of my students. In a Christian school where we are allowed to hug." She glared at the man in uniform, but he only shrugged.

"Doesn't matter. It's the rules." He adjusted his

important looking belt with the big buckle and winked. "I'll let it go this time, but remember, no hugging, no touching."

"But Santa is allowed? Makes no sense." She was angry and knew her face must be flushed with more color than Paris Red. She would address this situation with Colin when, if, she saw him again out of Santa uniform. That might be debatable considering how she felt about him right now. The cad.

The security officer started to steer her back to her Mrs. Santa position, but she had one more question. She noticed his badge said "Trainee." She didn't want to embarrass the young man, but he had embarrassed her. Had he overstepped the bounds in his job?

"Sir," she said wanting him to know she respected him, "the problem is that many of the next children coming to see Santa today will also be my students. They and their parents will recognize me. They will expect a hug. I can't ignore that. So," she looked him in the face, "what should I do? Be rude?" She waited a minute for her diatribe to process. "Surely the Santa company wouldn't want that. Would it?"

The poor man stepped aside. "Gotta call boss."

She waited, hoping "boss" was Colin. After all it was his company. Several minutes passed and she wondered about the other children visiting Santa. She knew most Kindergarteners were on the cusp of being too old to believe in the bearded elf. But moms and dads still wanted the pictures for posterity. Even for their own precious memories and their Christmas cards. She couldn't blame them. She kept a photo album of Tabitha growing up from birth to now. Jennifer probably did, too. But Patti would gift it to Tabby as part of her inheritance someday. From her Grammy.

The young man came back. He looked sheepish, and she felt sorry for him. Until . . .

"Sorry, Ma'am, but the powers that be say no touching, no hugging. I tried."

"You did your best. Now, I will do mine." She pulled her cellphone out of the voluminous skirt pocket and pushed the right buttons. If he didn't answer she would push redial over and over. She was so sure the current Santa was not Colin, and he shouldn't be sitting on the Santa throne. He'd better answer. Soon. Or after her job was over today she was going to confront him. In person.

Eighteen

Colin opened the door.

"What are you doing here? How did you find me" Colin's face was as white as his fake Santa beard, when he wore it.

"Probably same way you found me. The forms we filled out for the Mrs. Santa job."

"Oh, hadn't thought about that. So, what do you want?"

"I want to know . . ." She hesitated. How should she list them, the many offenses? She took a deep cleansing breath, stood tall and mimicked his posture when he had practically forced his way into her home. "I won't even graciously ask if I can come in. I am coming in."

Patti had a mental list in her head. Teachers did that. She spied what looked like his favorite chair, a recliner, and settled herself in it. She hated recliners. Old men chairs, lazy men chairs. But lifting the thingy at the end to elevate her feet did feel good. Especially after nine hours sweating in green vinyl boots.

"You settled?" His question was rhetorical, but she nodded and smiled.

"So?" Was the man totally clueless? Must be when he asked, "How was your day?"

Patti thought she would explode. In mirth, anger, frustration? She clenched her fists and made a conscience decision. Anger would get her nowhere, especially since he had no clue about her situation at the mall, even though he should have as the owner of the Santa Extravagancia Company, or whatever it was called. Yes, she was frustrated, but what else is new? After blowing out three deep breaths she burst into raucous laughter.

"You don't know?" She looked at his blank expression. "No, you really don't know, do you?"

So she told him.

~

Patti collapsed on her bed with clothes still on. At least she had changed from the ridiculous Mrs. Santa attire into her comfy lavender sweats before she went to Colin's. Not that he noticed. She admitted to herself Colin was mature, well, "older." He must have been romantic and in love at one time. How else could he have become a grandpa to Braydon and three other children? Maybe she needed to walk him through Romance 101. Maybe too late. She hoped not.

She twittled her thumbs trying to figure out how to reach him, especially for Braydon's sake. He came on way too strong toward the boy. She suspected Braydon was a very smart kid, but with some vague learning disability. She wondered if she could ask further. No, that was not her place. Instead, she prayed for the boy, the grandpa and the situation. God would see to it.

~

She awoke next morning with a pain in her neck. She wanted to think it was from her pillow and sleeping so tensely. But she suspected it was from her latest dream. Colin was dragging her to stand up in her Mrs. Santa costume beside him as Santa. Children from her Kindergarten class lined up, but she wasn't allowed to touch them, not even acknowledge them, only smile. Just before the dream ended, of course when she woke up, a bulky security guard led her away behind the curtain. When she slapped him in the face she woke up.

She had a faint recollection of Braydon and Tabitha being in the dream, too. She remembered images of the two children high-fiving. Did that mean they were friends? Or could be? Or were they glad she'd been dragged away by the security guard? Maybe they were happy she slapped him. She tried to recall the details of the dream and gave up.

Sipping her morning coffee she thought about that. They were both good kids, kids who respected their elders. Maybe their part in the dream was reassuring her. Or, could it have been a plea for help?

~

Patti felt bold. Bold enough to ask Colin about Braydon. But she needed to do it in person. She needed to see his face when she asked. How could she do that without being intrusive? Or having the man think she was enamored with him? She "sucked it up" as Tabby would say, then wondered where in the world did kids get those expressions.

Yet the words said what was meant.

She finally *sucked it up* to ask him to meet her at what had become their favorite Starbuck's place. That seemed innocuous enough. Not too personal, but somewhere they had met before on a comfortable friendly basis. She dialed.

"What's this about? We have nothing to say to each other anymore."

Whoa. What was this man's problem? She hadn't expected him to be so confrontational. She needed to diffuse his verbose rhetoric. But how?

"Well, Colin, I will be there in twenty minutes. You decide if you want to join me. Choice is yours." She took one of her cleansing breaths hoping he could hear the blowing out part. "What, what," she repeated, "happened to Mr. Jovial Santa. Bah, Humbug to you." She took another cleansing breath as she clicked off her phone. Once again she wished she'd called on the landline so she could slam the receiver down.

Patti knew she was in a huff. It would take her the twenty minutes driving to Starbucks to calm down. She pulled into an empty parking space next to the last empty handicap one. At least it was almost as close and she didn't have to fish her plastic thingy out of her purse.

She struggled getting out of the car and placed both feet squarely on the blacktop. Finally balanced, she locked the door with a click and walked slowly toward Safeway. No one was in line at her favorite Starbucks. As a bonus Sidney was the barista. Nice girl who remembered her customers.

"Hi, Mrs. Andrews. Where's Tabitha?"

"Left her home today. Too much sugar in the drink she orders," she quipped.

"You want your usual yummy latte? Cold or hot?"

"Cold today, Sidney. Need the cold to pick me up."

"Something wrong, Mrs. Andrews?"

"No. Well sort of." Sidney was a clever girl; told her the other day she was twenty-one. In college studying science something. Memorizing complicated ingredients that went into a plethora of drinks was probably right up her alley. Patti knew she could never do that. Science had never been her strong subject. She remembered in freshman year she'd rubbed the back of her lab partner in exchange for editing his English term paper while he did the science experiment on the poor frog. She opened her mouth to speak and ask for Sidney's youthful advice when she heard a gravelly voice behind her.

"You done ordering? My turn?"

Colin almost pushed her aside and in doing so got her elbow in his ribs. That, she decided, was tit for tat, or maybe Divine Intercession. Or Interference. Whichever, she would take it. He stooped slightly and wrapped his arms around his chest stifling a moan.

"And, hello to you, too, Colin," she said brightly. "You okay?" She almost had to hug her own chest to hold the mirth. The man was insufferable. What on earth did she see in him? Why bother?

She carried her latte to her favorite round

corner table, clasped her hands in her lap and waited with a smile on her face.

Nineteen

The conversation hadn't gone too badly. Or maybe it had. She hated stubborn people, men especially. Mr. Fancy Santa was certainly one. Yet, when she thought about how Colin welcomed the children, especially the other day when he took over from Grumpy Santa and played the role, her heart did a warm flutter. But thinking back her mind was filled with questions. Why had he seemed different yesterday? She'd worked with Colin the first week, so she thought she knew his persona. He hadn't looked different, except for the extra rosy cheeks. But he'd had a cold. Still his nose hadn't run and he'd never asked for nor pulled out a tissue to wipe. Of course the entire Santa facade was a fake, but had that one been an even faker Santa? Was that Santa really Colin? Everything about him had been the same, even his warmth toward the children. The "Ho, ho, hos" sounded genuine. The fake beard looked the same, the moustache was in place. Then she remembered.

For some crazy reason their breaks alternated and did not occur at the same time. Maybe so someone, either Mrs. Santa or the supposedly jolly elf was always present to reassure kids and parents. When Santa returned from his break and she took hers, they had passed each other briefly. She remembered he'd had one of his Santa gloves off. But just before he pulled it back on she had reached out to clasp his hand. It was smooth. It baffled her since Colin's were dry and rough the few times she'd touched them. Maybe he'd had a manicure with a paraffin treatment. She sometimes got those on her feet after a pedicure. The result was always velvet smooth skin for at least the rest of the day. Colin could have gone to a salon early that morning. Lots of macho males get manicures and pedicures. Whenever she was at Kay's getting hers there were often several men. Usually older men like Colin, or athletes, or doctors in hospital scrubs. Those were the men who either had the confidence to get pampered or had a real reason to – like the docs who scoured their hands many times a day, especially if they were surgeons. Mmm. Maybe she should ask him. It would be fun, even bonding, to sit next to each other in pedi chairs. Instead they were sitting across a table from each other in Starbucks.

He'd finally joined her with his decaf latte. No whipped cream or cinnamon floated on top. She'd pondered making a snide remark about that, but decided that would only set him more on edge. The man really needed to get a life.

"So," he grumbled, "why am I here? Something wrong?"

"Well, no, yes, sort of."

"How difficult is it for you to decide? Is it a

teacher thing?"

She laughed. Maybe he was right. "Maybe it is, but not this time. I want to talk about Braydon." His face did that blanching thing.

"What did he do now? The boy has no, how you say, 'filter.' No sense of what is appropriate. What did he do now?" he repeated. That was another thing that annoyed her, repeating himself. Maybe he had taken a Toastmasters class. She knew pastors often repeated phrases to make a point. Or, maybe he thought she was hard of hearing.

Before she could respond he started to make more apologies for his grandson.

She reached across the table to touch his hand briefly and drew hers away. His was still dry, crackly, rough. Trying to set that aside, she focused on what she hoped would be a positive discussion about Braydon. She would deal with the hand thing later.

She explained that her minor in psychology, though rusty, and her years of experience as a teacher gave her some insight into children's behavior.

"Colin," she said as she reached for his hand again and swallowed hard at the roughness with a grimace, "are you familiar with First Corinthians Thirteen? In the Bible?"

"Is that the one about through a glass darkly?"

"Spot on. Yes."

"How does that apply to Braydon?"

"I think it applies perfectly." She waited for his huge, sputtering sigh to subside and wiped up the coffee he'd spilled on the table with extra napkins.

Good thing she'd grabbed a wad of them.

"I think, and please Colin hear me out, I think Braydon has a learning disability. A minor one, but one that impairs his social skills. Reading skills, too. Sometimes they overlap with the child's frustrations."

She wadded her hands in her lap praying for the stubborn man to understand.

"What's wrong with him?"

"Nothing is 'wrong' with him. He is obviously a smart kid with a great personality."

"So, why does he say the wrong things at the wrong time? Why does he embarrass me?"

Patti bit her lip. So sad Colin was embarrassed by that sweet boy. She hoped her next words took root.

"Colin, I want you to listen carefully. Please." He looked troubled, but nodded. That was a start.

"Thousands of children have some minor learning or cognitive disabilities. Actually, they shouldn't be labeled that way. They are cognitive 'differences.' Just like our eye colors and skin colors are different. Even if we are from the same gene pool. Siblings are good examples." She paused for a breath, and to be sure he was paying attention. She hoped she wasn't addressing him like she talked to her Kindergarten students. She wanted him to understand, not resent her words. Finally she asked, "Does Braydon look exactly like his siblings?"

"No," he shook his head. "All three girls have brownish hair. His, as you know, is blond." She nodded.

"You mentioned he's very smart in math and chess."

"Yeh, but he has trouble reading - sometimes. Mostly comprehension. Stares at words too long, can't focus on what he reads, doesn't understand some words. Even says they don't make sense. But," he twirled his paper cup making rings on the table, "he's been tested for dyslexia. So it's not that."

"Auditory processing."

"What? That would be listening, right? He hears just fine."

"Well, some kind of processing." She squinted her eyes to think. "It has something to do with the written word, especially if he has no trouble with numbers and has no spatial misconceptions. If he is so good in math and can figure out moves several times ahead in chess . . ." Her voice trailed off.

Twenty

Patti had a restless night. She hated those, had always prided herself she could fall sound asleep in a wink. Instead last night the wink became a blink, and a blink, and many more blinks. She wasn't sure why she was so disturbed about Braydon's problem now that Colin and she had become friendly again. She loved the boy for his cleverness and energy, she felt committed to figure out Braydon's problem. Mostly because Colin was so frustrated with it. She understood his frustration, even his occasional anger. But she suspected a lot of both were really Colin's to himself for not understanding or helping the boy. Why did grandparents have to be the ones to solve kid problems?

They were meeting again at Starbucks before today's Santa gig. She'd donned her Mrs. costume to be ready in time. Colin, lucky man, could wait to change behind the curtain. He didn't have to disrobe, just pull on a red velour suit, boots and beard over his normal attire. The outfit actually made him look a bit stockier, more "Santa-y". Yesterday she mentioned, half in jest, half serious, it would be a great promotional appearance if they both showed up at Starbucks in costume.

"No way!" he protested.

She hiked up her green skirt and fastened the Velcro under the fake buttons on her vest. The silly cap and wire-rimmed glasses stayed in her voluminous purse.

This time he was punctual and had ordered her special drink. What a guy! A guy who didn't believe in ordinary salutations, like "Hi!"

He shoved the drink toward her splashing some on the table. She wiped with the napkins she'd grabbed when she came in. It had become a predictable routine.

"Did you find anything out? About Braydon's problem?"

"Good morning to you, too, Colin." She deliberately folded her hands and rested them on her red skirt.

"Sorry. Hi!"

"To answer your question, no, not exactly." She hoped her smile diffused his frown.

"Didn't think so. You're not a shrink."

"No, I'm not, Colin. But you are a very impatient man. I did the best I could by Googling and reading.

"I do have some ideas and more information to explore. I hope you know I care a lot about Braydon, a whole lot. I am doing the best I can."

~

I can't do this. Can I do this? Thoughts spun around in her head. Had she taken on more than she could handle? Caring was one thing, helping was another.

Today the Santa experience was going with no hitches, no former students of Patti's. Just random kids. Five minutes to go and she could rush home to remove the ridiculous bonnet and the silly costume that was making her sweat. She was sure there were little moons under her arms on her blouse. She felt them. But avoided checking. That would be too obvious.

A sigh escaped her mouth, until a shrill voice caught her attention.

Twenty-one

"What are you doing? What kind of dad and grandpa are you? You are a mockery, a fake!"

Patti wasn't sure if she should intervene, but she was sure who the woman was. Just as she took a tentative step forward the straggly-haired blonde lunged for her.

Patti protectively crossed her arms and raised them to her face in an automatic gesture. The incensed woman came at her with arms flailing. Just before she was about to hit Patti another voice took over.

"Stop, Miranda, stop!" Colin's deep voice was clear and loud.

Santa descended from his throne and wrapped his bulky arms around the woman. Fortunately, the signs had already been placed saying "Santa will be back tomorrow at 10 a.m. See you then. Ho, Ho."

~

"I need a foot massage. Maybe a pedicure from Tammy."

How many times, how often, she wondered had

she talked to herself in the mirror? Never had the glass answered. She kept trying.

"I know it's silly, Lord. But it helps me focus and figure out problems. Thanks for listening."

Crawling into bed she prayed that tonight she really would sleep.

~

Dang that phone! She was sure she'd turned it off. Oh, the landline. Craning her neck to the bedside table she saw the notice on the little screen – Jefferson Colin. She picked up the receiver reluctantly.

"Yes?"

"Sorry, it's only nine-thirty. You go to bed early?"

"Colin, nine-thirty is not early. What can I do for you?" She prided herself she didn't yell and ask "What do you want?"

"Want to tell you about a change in scene tomorrow. That's all. Good night."

She stared at the receiver in her hand and put it back on its stand. She didn't know how to turn it off, or if she could. And she was too tired to figure out how to slam it down.

She sighed and prayed for sleep. But it didn't come.

Men!

Patti punched her pillow and flipped it over. "I got myself into this mess," she announced to the dark in her bedroom. "And now I'm talking to myself. Ugh."

She knew her biggest dilemma was the boy. What could she do to help Braydon, and his grandpa? What did Colin mean "A change of venue"? When no answers came, she finally drifted off.

Twenty-two

It was still dark outside at 5:30 in the morning. Winter had finally appeared in Arizona. She was sipping her coffee by the dim light under the microwave. The overhead light in the kitchen was too glaring, at least until she woke up more. The shrill sound of the phone startled her and the mug shook in her hand splashing brown liquid across the glass table top.

"Yikes! What now?" she said reaching for a paper towel to mop up the mess. Soggy paper still in hand she grabbed the receiver just as the annoying voice started to announce, "Ander . . ."

"Do you know what time it is?" She knew her voice was laced with sarcasm, but really couldn't he have waited until after six?

"Sorry," he mumbled. But he didn't sound sorry. "No Santa at the store today. I called us both in sick."

"What! Why? I'm not sick. You?"

"Uh, no. But there is a minor emergency we have to fill in for."

"What kind of emergency, where?"

"At PCH."

"What's that? Oh, the kids' hospital?"

"Yes, Phoenix Children's. I'm on the board. Got a call last night from the woman who's the event coordinator, Janette somebody. It's family portrait day with Santa, and their Santa is sick."

"Of course we have to help. But I don't like the fact you lied to the store. I'm sure they would understand."

"No, they're a business. But I do have an idea. And I only said Santa is sick. Didn't say which Santa where." He chuckled. "Lie of omission."

"But, Colin, I'm not sick. So you lied about me."

"That's what's called, well . . . a projected lie." She could hear the smirk in his voice and another almost silent chuckle. "I know your kind heart, Patti, so figured you would be sick, at least at heart, if those children were disappointed. And," he almost whispered, "I have a backup plan."

"You scoundrel!"

"Sometimes, yes." This time he guffawed. "Can you be ready by seven-thirty? I will pick you up. Traffic will be heavy then."

"I'll have to rush. But yes, I can."

She hung up and mopped up the rest of her spilled coffee. "Gotta hurry," she told her reflection in the microwave door. "That man is so frustrating." She stuck out her tongue and held her nose. That made her feel better. Maybe she would do that to Colin when he picked her up. *Wonder what his Plan B is.*

~

Colin had the radio up loud when the morning

news flash came on.

"I'm not deaf!" she shouted.

"Shh. Want to hear the traffic report. Calm down."

"Detour Dan here," the peppy voice announced. "Twenty-three minutes on the I17 – two crashes there, but off to the right. One on the 101South at Hayden, but off to the left. Still, allow extra time. Traffic is backed up. Not bad for this time of the morning.

"Now for the surface streets. Uh oh. A minor scuffle just off the 101North at the Cave Creek exit. Just a fender bender. A cyclist involved accident on Shea Boulevard at a Hundred and Second Street. Looks like a child. Detour Dan signing off. This traffic report was brought to you by King Plumbing. If you have plumbing problems call the King at 1-800-tripple two, 3330."

Patti gripped Colin's arm. "That's just down the street."

"That's the way Braydon rides his bike to school." He made a U-turn at the Ninety-sixth Street light and doubled back. His face looked like it was carved in stone.

"I pray it isn't him. Even so," she said, "we should check. Especially if it's a child."

His slight nod was reassuring. She hoped he was praying like she was.

All northbound traffic was stopped. Two cars were angled strangely, one behind the other, at the intersection. A woman wearing a baseball cap was standing at the open door of a tan SUV talking on her cellphone and gesturing. A man sat on the curb with his head in his hands. A small body was sprawled on the pavement near him with another man leaning over it and pressing on its chest.

"Oh, God, please no." Patti's voice warbled. Colin gripped her hand and squeezed.

They were climbing out of his car when they heard the whine of a siren. Then another louder one. A police car pulled up beside them and an officer waved them back just as a paramedic fire truck angled in front of their car.

"Uh," he hesitated. "Step back, please, sir, madam." He peered at them and said, "Who are you?"

"Officer," Colin forced his way toward the uniformed man. "That might be my grandson." He pointed to the form sprawled on the sidewalk.

"Name and license, sir, uh Santa." Patti noticed the cop's lips curled up a bit. How unprofessional! Then she remembered Colin's and her apparel and noticed the woman on the cellphone was taking pictures of them. They must look a sight. At least Colin wasn't wearing his fake beard, and she hadn't donned the silly bonnet. Still, how often did Santa and his Mrs. show up at accidents?

Colin reached in his back pocket and pulled out his wallet. The officer was still trying to control his face as he looked at Colin's identification and nodded. "What's the boy's name?"

"Braydon."

The policeman walked over to the prone child and leaned down. He seemed to be checking the plastic card hanging from the child's neck.

"It's the kid's ID for school," Colin said when

Patti looked questioningly at him. "Doesn't Tabby wear one?"

"Yes. I forgot. Just nervous."

Another car pulled up and screeched to a grinding halt. A woman with wild blonde hair jumped out and ran toward the child. She bent down sobbing and cradled his head.

"Please don't do that, Ma'am. He could have a head injury and that could make it worse."

She glared at the paramedic with tears running down her face. "But he's my boy. I have to hold my boy."

The paramedic nodded to his left and a female officer placed her hands on the woman's arms and pulled her back. She collapsed in the officer's arms sobbing.

"It is him, isn't it?" Patti asked Colin. "That's your daughter, right?"

Colin nodded and gripped her hand again, this time tighter. Now it was her turn to sob. She hunched over and felt strong arms around her.

~

Santa and Mrs. C. assist police in accident of child.

The headline was above the picture of her and Colin in their Santa attire. On the front page. Must not have had any other important story. Fortunately it didn't give any names, not theirs or Braydon's. Maybe a young inexperienced reporter. Even as a weekly columnist for a local paper years ago she would never have let that slide. It did say where children could meet these particular Santa impersonators. Oh, well, Monday would probably bring an onslaught of looky-loos.

Twenty-three

Patti collapsed on the trundle bed in the guest room. Colin was stretched out on her sofa. They were both exhausted. Colin had called the children's hospital while she made coffee that neither drank. She picked up her cup and shuffled into the living room. He looked so calm with his long frame taking up all available space. *He really is cute. For an older man.*

She carefully set her cup on the side table with her favorite *Do All Things With Love* coaster under it. No more spilled coffee for her. She debated waking him, but just then he stirred.

"The other Santa," he said, "wasn't really all that sick."

"What?"

"Yeh, he had a bad hemorrhoid problem. Used his salve, and when he heard about our state of affairs, he showed up." He covered his mouth – to avoid a laugh?

Patti couldn't help it. Her laugh bubbled up from her tummy to her throat then spilled out. "THAT was his problem?" she managed to ask between spates of laughter.

Colin nodded, laughing. "Guess so. Kind of a woos."

Suddenly they both got serious.

"Braydon! We should go NOW!"

"No. Actually, it's okay not to. Miranda is with him. He's recovered consciousness, talking, even laughing. Apparently, he was doing what boys do and tried to make a wheelie to get on the curb after he crossed the street." He raised his brows and rolled his eyes.

Patti noticed the quiver of his lips and slapped her thigh. "That stinker!" she snickered. "But praise God he wasn't seriously hurt."

"Well," Colin said, "he does have some scrapes and bruises, although he undoubtedly deserves them. I hope he learned his lesson."

"Probably not," she replied. "I bet you did dumb stuff like that when you were a kid."

Colin looked at her crookedly and chuckled. "Who me? Of course . . . not. I was a perfect kid. It was my brother who did all the dumb stuff. At least that's what I told my mother."

She had finally found the perfect excuse to stick her tongue out at him. And laugh. He covered his eyes with his hands and laughed with her.

"But," she suddenly got serious, "if Miranda is with him, what about the girls, his sisters?"

"Melissa, the eldest, is fourteen. Old enough to watch over the others. There's also Belinda their neighbor on call. It's okay. We can go tomorrow. If he's still there."

~

Patti held Colin's wrist. When he made a sound of pain, she noticed her fingernails had left imprints on his skin. "Sorry."

"Getting used to it," he said. "Not exactly a loving touch, but I'll take it."

"You will?" She hoped he would elaborate. When he didn't, she nudged him. "What did that comment mean, that you'd 'take it'?"

Placing his hands on her shoulders he turned her to face him. What was he doing? Suddenly she felt his lips on hers. A sort of smack. Loud, not quiet. Not romantic.

"What was that about?"

"Wanted to kiss you for a long time. Just got brave."

She would show him brave. She wiggled up close pressing herself against his chest and her lips tenderly on his. He gasped.

"How was that for brave?"

"Great!" He tipped her chin and pecked her nose. Grinning he asked, "Where do we go from here?"

Patti stepped back. "I don't know, Colin, but usually it's the guy who takes the lead. Do you have one?"

Twenty-four

"Grammy, is Braydon all right?"

Patti picked Tabitha up for their Sunday afternoon knitting lesson. What a blessing the hobby store where she and Colin now played Santa and Mrs. was closed on Sundays. How wonderful some retailers lived by their faith. They were going to Knit Picks, but wasn't that different? Was knitting working? She decided to not pursue the question. God would figure it out.

"It sounds like he will fully recover and be fine. Just needs some bedrest to be sure he doesn't have a concussion."

"I want to visit him."

Typical Tabby. No "Can I" or "May I" or "Is it possible."

"Not sure that's a good idea, Tab. I need to ask Mr. Colin about that."

"Ask, please."

~

Patti settled herself in the chair at Knit Picks and pulled her yarn out of her bag. This shouldn't be too hard. But her mind was nowhere near knitting. The yarn snagged on her thumb and the needle in her right hand slipped.

"Trouble, Grammy?" Tabby looked at her with wide eyes. "I can help you."

Patti handed her knitting disaster over to Tabby who corrected it in thirty seconds.

"See, Grammy, you just do this and this. Easy. You can do it."

Patti managed to complete the knitting assignment for today with Tabby's help. Oh, to be eleven again.

"I'm going to knit him a scarf."

"What? Who?"

"Braydon of course."

"How nice." So that was settled. At least in Tabby's mind. But not hers. Should she knit a scarf for Colin? Would that bring them closer together? Christmas was less than two weeks away.

They climbed in the car and fastened seat belts. Then Tabby exploded.

"I'm scared, Grams."

"Oh, dear, sweet girl. Of what?" Was the child being bullied at school? Was she afraid of her teachers? Were those horrible video games frightening her?

"Not of what, but for whom?" Tabby screwed up her innocent little face. Turning to Patti she said, "I'm scared for Braydon."

Whew. Hopefully a hurdle crossed.

"What do you mean scared FOR him? He is recovering nicely, and thankfully doesn't have a head injury."

"Well . . . he seems baffled, confused. Not from any injury, but something inside of him."

"Tabby, you haven't even seen him since his accident."

"I know, but I've been thinking about him a lot. And, I worry."

"Gracious, Tab. It's so nice of you to be concerned about a friend. But maybe you are being too introspective? Do you know what that word means?"

"Sort of." Tabby closed her eyes and squinted. "Thoughtful?"

"Yes. It could also mean considerate and caring." Patti took her hand off the steering wheel and laid it briefly on Tabitha's arm. "Maybe a little too much." She had posed it as a question, or had she?

"But, Grammy," Tabby twisted in her seat toward Patti, "you told me to care about others. Even told me to pray for them." She twisted back and stared ahead out of the windshield. "I have been praying for Braydon. So there."

Twenty-five

Patti yanked at the sheet twisting it around her shoulder. Fighting sleep was getting her nowhere, so she threw off the offending 500 plus thread-count cotton and made a cup of herb tea. Cradling the mug, again only sitting by the light of the microwave, she questioned.

What did Colin's kiss, and his comment about brave, mean? How really was Braydon? Why did his mother hate Patti? Had she done the right thing taking the Mrs. Santa job, or even applying for it? Was she too old to fall in love again? Was Colin?

A Bible verse, one she could barely remember, came to mind about how each day has troubles of its own, and not to worry ahead. One summer, when Jennifer was nine, she had agreed to volunteer as a fill-in Sunday school teacher for third and fourth graders. There had been thirteen boys in the class of twenty. Now she could probably handle them. But Mariners Church never asked her to teach a Sunday school class again. The memory made her giggle and her tea splashed on the table. More mopping up again, but this time she grabbed a kitchen towel.

She started with the Colin question. Was she ready for love again? Was he? Her heart pinged. Memories could be so painful. Or they could be sweet. She thought of the forty-five years of love she and Devin had shared. She had spent thirty-five of those years being a stay-at-home mom and a PTA volunteer doing everything she could to help "Plant the Seeds of Knowledge," one of the Parent, Teachers Associations slogans. When Devin retired they planned to conquer the world, or at least explore it. They had mapped out a five-year plan. Europe, Scandinavia, Costa Rica, and especially Banff, Canada where his parents had spent their honeymoon. It all sounded so romantic. Then one day in November when they had just left the bank with a bunch of Travelers Checks, when they were laughing and holding hands, Darrin said, "I'm sorry" as he fell to the pavement. It was that fast, that unexpected, but, somehow, he instantly knew. At least enough to apologize.

At first, she was angry at him. Did he know something about his health he hadn't shared? She had been clasping his hand, and suddenly he was lying on the sidewalk. The doctors, several of them, all specialists, confirmed he had been in excellent health until abruptly his heart gave out. She shoved aside the memories of her sons and Jennifer sobbing, of the funeral and all the pomp and circumstance, all his professional colleagues hugging her. In the end she did an outrageous thing and had "I'm sorry" engraved as an epitaph on his headstone. She knew he would get a kick out of that with his unconventional sense of humor.

Laughing aloud and pressing a tissue under her eyes she shook off the memories. Was she ready for love again? Was Colin? She knew so little about him, other than he was a Santa who cuddled children and a grandpa who cared. Surely God had orchestrated their situation. Hadn't the teen boy who'd collected the application she'd filled out for Mrs. Santa looked at her in a strange way and said, "Good luck"? Silly thought, and she didn't believe in superstition. But she did believe in signs. The Bible had many. Maybe she should get back to reading the Word every morning. That, and to find out more about Colin.

~

She Googled. She hated looking people up. Products were okay. She'd only done a person once before when she was confused about something her pastor brought up in a sermon. The man turned out to almost be a saint. But then the Bible says all believers are saints. So confusing.

Colin David Anderson wasn't listed as a saint, but he was lauded for being an honest businessman. Santa Extravaganza was a triple Better Business Bureau star. Had been for over a dozen years. Why had she never heard of it before? Maybe because she'd never thought about those mall and store Santas. Just trusted. It had been founded by Colin and his brother Caleb.

She remembered the biblical Caleb from when he scouted the giants in the Bible. He was the one who had devotion to God. He was one of the ten, and only one of the two who claimed the giants in Canaan could be defeated. But David was the one who defeated Goliath. Maybe that's why Colin's middle name is David. She looked again. Both men's middle names were David. How odd.

Twenty-six

Monday. Mrs. Santa again. She didn't like dressing up as someone else. She had loved Halloween years ago when she had taken Jennifer around in the community. She was always a clown, had the costume packed away for the next year. That was fun, especially because Jennifer looked so cute every year whether she was a Disney character or her costume had been contrived from hand downs. Her favorite was Jennifer as Raggedy Ann. She had looked so adorable, even carried a Raggedy Ann doll. Thank goodness it was now Jennifer's responsibility to take Tabby. She wasn't sure what Tabby had dressed as this year because the girl had changed her mind at least a dozen times. Some character from a video game? Probably a costume from the racks, not like the ones Patti had laboriously hand made. Those were special.

So much had changed.

She powdered her eyebrows and pulled up the silly skirt to adjust it around her waist. The waist she kept meaning to go to the gym for but never seemed to have the time. That's when her cellphone buzzed.

"I want to come, Grammy."

The girl had no filter. Yes she was bright, yes she was eleven, but what about "May I come today with you?"

"Tabby, isn't this a school day? You need to be in class."

"Nope. Well, sort of. It's a half day, an inservice day for teachers. They call it an early release day. I get out at noon. Mom says she can drive me to the hobby store. I still have my elf costume. Okay?"

It would be fun to have Tabby at her side, as long as the girl didn't confiscate a camera. Patti chuckled remembering the incident when Tabby wanted to help the mother. Sadly, it put the mother back in jail and her children in foster care again. She looked forward to having Tabitha next to her as a cute elf helper. She felt as if she needed all the help she could get.

~

What was wrong?

Dozens of people, mostly women and small children, were lined up and mumbling and shifting in place. Where was Colin? He was always so prompt.

Today was a late day for Santa photos. It had been in the newspaper and online. Maybe not everyone had read or heard about it. There was an even more ridiculous online thing where parents could purchase tickets and print them out to give them priority as one of the first in line, at least privileged. Now she would have to take tickets as well as credit cards. So much to figure out. Maybe

Tabby could help her.

"What can I do, Grammy, to help?" Tabitha had shown up right on time at twelve-fifteen and bustled her way through the crowd. "I'm an elf," she said, as she tried to push people aside. Others smiled and left space for her. Maybe it was the costume or her confident voice. Whatever it was it worked.

"Just smile and look cute." Patti knew Tabby could do that.

Patti adjusted her own cap with the silly trim on it, pushed the fake glasses down on her nose, and grinned. Where was Colin? No Santa.

She heard grumbling behind the curtain, and it suddenly parted. Whew! Just in time.

Again Colin looked different. His cheeks were redder and his Santa belly was more ponderous, more real. Not the fake one Colin usually padded with a pillow. Had he gained weight overnight?

Patti didn't have time to contemplate, the children pushed forward and she kept pushing the button on the credit card device. Tabby opened her arms and welcomed each child with a grin and "I'm Santa's elf here to help." The kids loved that. She even said to some, "I will remind him you want a . . ."

The day was almost over and the line had thinned. Thank goodness, because Patti was tired and her feet ached in the green plastic boots. Ten more minutes to go. Even Tabby's exuberance had faded. She still opened her arms wide and smiled, but her smile was wobbly.

Patti was about to put up the sign – Thank you

for visiting Santa. He will be here tomorrow at 10 a.m. She fiddled with the post it was on. No Santa to help her. He'd bailed at seven on the dot. So much for depending on Colin, or whomever Santa was. The cad.

Tabby helped her set the sign up and stabilize it. Walking to their car she blurted out, "Why wasn't Mr. Colin the Santa, Grammy?"

Twenty-seven

"Uh, uh . . . he was."

"No he wasn't. He looked kind of the same, sort of. But different." Tabitha kept shaking her head all the way to the car. "Nope. Not Mr. Colin."

"What makes you say that, Tabby? Tell me what you think was different about him."

"His cheeks. Too red. His eyes – not twinkling. His laugh was different, too. Fake. Not like Mr. Colin's laugh. Not warm." She stopped walking and put a finger to her nose. "Aha! He smelled different."

"He did? How so?"

"Mr. Colin smells good. This Santa smelled like that drugstore smell, that cheap one."

"How do you know about that?"

"'cause Daddy used to wear it 'till Mommy complained." She grinned up at Patti. "Now Mom orders one from the internet."

~

"This is getting old."

Patti stirred her tea with honey and herbs while clanking the spoon against the mug. She and Tabby had had a late dinner at Chick-fil-A, not her usual

101

dining experience. But the salad with the avocado and lime dressing was just right, and Tabby devoured six nuggets, French fries and a large coke. The child deserved it, especially for her astute observations about the cad. Patti had wished she was eleven again and could consume that many calories and be that thin. After she'd dropped Tabby off at her home she felt disconjointed. Or was it discombobulated? Whatever.

Now she was echoing Colin's favorite word. What was wrong with her? Maybe she should see a shrink. What did the kids say? "Get a life." Or was that from her era? She added more honey to her tea and stirred vigorously until it splashed over the cup. More mopping up needed. Just as she grabbed a kitchen towel her cellphone rang.

Not answering. Nope. Whatever. She grinned and snubbed her nose in the air to Mr. Whatever.

Next came a text bing. Nope, not responding.

She sat back down at her table and stirred the liquid in her cup again. She would be strong.

She rinsed out her cup, locked the door and climbed the stairs to bed.

"Good night, Mr. Whatever," she said into the air while snubbing her nose again.

~

Five-thirty again! Did that man never sleep? She pulled the sleep mask off and picked up the phone.

"What's the emergency this time?"

"Church needs a Santa."

"What church doesn't?"

"My, our, church. Tomorrow right after the

eight-thirty service."

"Why then?"

"That's the service they bring the needy kids to. The one we've all been donating presents to."

Patti tried to remember. Had she donated? She always had in years past, choosing at least three requests from the trees in the foyer. Of course being a preschool teacher she loved buying a gift for a small child. But teens and preteens didn't get chosen as often, so she always picked one of them, even though without Tabby's help she never knew what to buy. The last choice was random. Yes, she remembered. A child, actually a teen, in state custody. How awful was that? Would anyone else choose him?

"Tell me the time and the attire. I will be there. Whenever," she added. She almost added "Whatever." But she didn't want to give him the satisfaction.

~

"This is so much fun, Grammy. I'm excited."

Tabitha pulled her forward, obviously not embarrassed about her grandmother being in Mrs. Santa attire. Patti tugged at her skirt.

"Don't worry, Grams. You look terrific. SO Mrs. Santa."

Patti thought Tabby could have a career in PR. The girl was a natural.

The community center of the church was filled with bodies. What was that smell? Oops, human smell. She made her way to the stage where Pastors Judith and Terry were talking. Someone gave her a hand to help her climb the steep steps. Tabby still held her hand tight and looked around.

"He's not here, Grammy." Suddenly she said, "But you are. You go, Grammy, go!"

A huge mound of wrapped and unwrapped gifts was piled around her feet. She had trouble navigating them. Finally, she was led to a high stool she almost jumped to sit on with the help of two young pastors. She gathered the Mrs. Santa skirt she hated around her knees and tugged at the silly cap.

"Good morning, everyone. As you see I am Mrs. Santa. As with many women I organize and delegate and put everything into motion." Loud clapping almost deafened her. "This is Elf Tabby who is here to help me." Tabby grinned and opened her arms. More clapping. Maybe the children liked the idea that a child was Santa's helper. She hoped so.

"Santa Claus had a setback and is a bit late. I'm sure he will be here soon." More clapping, more smiles. Apparently, the audience of mostly children didn't care who gave out the gifts, just so they got them. She did notice mothers shushing children and trying to quiet them. The children seemed desperate for the presents. How sad.

Tabby was an only child, as Patti had been. Neither had siblings to share with, but both were generous. At least she hoped so. Many of the children in the audience had siblings squeezing in next to them. She realized had no instruction about how to distribute the gifts. How should she do it?

Always to the rescue, Tabby whispered in her ear.

"It's a lottery system, Grammy. A random

drawing. Each child has a number." She handed Patti a bucket filled with crumpled bits of paper. "Just draw one at a time and announce the number. The child whose number you draw gets to run up to the stage and choose a gift from the pile."

"But what if the number is for a teenager and the gift he or she chooses is for a five year old?"

"The church leaders in charge of this figured that out. The pile of gifts to your left are for older kids, the big pile at your feet are for little kids. Keep a wary eye and try to guide them to the right pile."

"A wary eye, huh? Where did you learn that wording?"

Tabitha grinned. "From you, Grammy."

Music played in the background. The Little Drummer Boy sounded just right for the occasion. Patti pulled a scrap of paper from the bucket, held the microphone that had been handed to her and announced, "Number 213. Please come choose a Santa gift."

Twenty-eight

How was she supposed to end this? Over three hundred children had chosen gifts. There were no piles left at her feet. She didn't see any teary-eyed cheeks or mothers trying to console little ones. Should she apologize for the missing Santa? Where was the cad?

Just as she was about to wiggle off the ridiculously high stool, she heard a loud "Ho, Ho, Ho."

He burst into the room with arms spread wide and a huge fake grin on his face. Patti saw immediately his beard was slipping. Just slightly, but maybe not enough to have even the youngest children notice. Fortunately, no child made a comment, and no child tried to grasp it or tug it as he made his way through the crowd. She finally slid off her high stool and spread her own arms wide. He had finally appeared.

"Welcome to Santa, everyone!"

The children gathered around him hoping for a touch of his magic. Because it was her job Patti spread her arms again and clasped his gloved hand for a show of enthusiasm. But she didn't feel it.

The crowd finally dispersed. Everyone seemed happy, laughing and talking. The gifting to the children was a success. No thanks to the cad.

Alone in the worship center, the two in their disguises stood face to face. Santa's beard had slipped more. Patti knew her skirt had slipped a few inches, too, but it still held in place with the elastic waist. Hands at her side she was conflicted until suddenly she got courage. She flung her arms around Santa's neck and kissed him full on the lips.

"So," she said, "finally you made it." He looked puzzled. "Thanks for leaving me in the lurch, you cad."

"Who are you?" the bearded man asked. "Not that I didn't like the affection."

Patti felt a tug on her arm. "Grammy, wrong Santa."

"Oh, my. Really?"

"Yep. Certain." Tabby's grin was infectious. When she started to giggle, Patti burst out laughing. What had she done?

She turned to the man with the naturally white eyebrows. Colin had to powder his dark ones. But these were obviously at least pale gray. Covering her mouth and nose with her hands she finally had the courage to ask, "Who are YOU?"

Before he could answer Braydon raced up the aisle of the church and threw his arms around the man's big Santa belly.

"Hi, Uncle Caleb! So great you're here. Sorry Grandpa couldn't make it."

"Hey, Bray," Tabby said loudly, "let's go get some of that hot cocoa the church promised to have for the kids. It's supposed to be in the Sunday school room." Just before Tabitha tugged his arm and pulled him away she leaned toward Patti. "Make it right, Grammy," she whispered. "You can do it."

Twenty-nine

Patti put more honey in her bedtime tea. She was getting very tired of this routine. Maybe she should add a splash of brandy like her mother used to do. Couldn't hurt.

She rose to find the ancient bottle when her phone rang. Dang. Again not on the landline. How she wanted to slam it down. Hard to do that with a cellphone. Not finding the bottle of brandy she pushed the green talk button to accept the call.

"I suppose you want to apologize for not showing up and leaving it all to me."

"Nope. Want an apology from you for kissing my brother. He said it was pretty amazing."

Sputtering was not normal for Patti, but when she finally got control of her lips and her tongue, she took a deep breath and spoke. "You are a cad!" With that she pushed the red button and put her phone on silent.

She ignored the ringing of the landline phone and kept stirring her tea. She opened the bottle of caramel colored liquid she finally found hidden behind the cake mixes. The brandy, and the sherry beside it, were designated for the holiday cakes she baked to share with neighbors. She knew alcohol was supposed to burn off during cooking according to Food Network Recipes, and the liqueurs were supposed to get better with age, but the scent overwhelmed her. Screwing the lid back on she shoved the bottle to the back of the pantry drawer. Maybe next time she would use lemon and orange flavoring in her special cakes.

~

Tabby called the next morning. Patti knew from the caller ID it was Jennifer's number so she answered.

"So, Grammy, did you get it all straightened out?"

"Not exactly, Tab. You were right about the wrong Santa. It was Mr. Colin's brother."

"I know. Don't know how, just knew. Did you ask him about it?" Patti could visualize Tabby's expression – eyebrows raised, lips puckered, nose wrinkled.

"Didn't need to. He called and asked me to apologize for kissing his brother. The nerve!"

"Well, I hope you didn't, Grammy. Apologize I mean. How would you know?"

The English major and teacher almost kicked in. Tempted to correct Tabby's use of present tense and explain it should be past tense, she shook her head. What was wrong with her? She was getting off track.

"What do you think I should do?" Was she really asking an eleven-year-old?

She heard the "Mmm" on the other end. Then Tabby spoke firmly.

"I think you should start with a non-issue about your friendship with Mr. Colin."

"Like?"

"Maybe Braydon?" Patti heard a short huff. "I can help with that." Tabby sounded so positive, so she listened to the girl's idea.

She knew it was a good place to start, from the beginning. Why was Tabby so smart? Why was she taking the advice of a child? Then she remembered Jesus' words about having the little children come unto Him.

"Here's my idea," Tabby explained.

"Okay. I can do that. You sure?"

"Very sure, Grammy. I like Braydon a lot and want to help him. I know I can," she said confidently.

~

"Well, here goes," she said to the little screen on the phone and dialed.

"No, Colin, I am not calling to apologize for a simple mistake." She took a breath when she heard only silence. That man! "I am calling for Tabby. She is requesting a playdate with Braydon."

They decided on Starbucks again. Made sense she thought when she settled into the round corner table the next day. Christmas was only two days away. She hadn't made her famous cakes, nor even decorated her tree. She had tried to pull the ancient artificial one out of the garage cabinet. Too cumbersome. It was the one Devin gave her for their last Christmas together. A cheap one from Big Lots. Devin was never extravagant with gifts, just remembered things she'd taken a shine to.

They had just settled into the round table when Tabby asked if she and Braydon could move to another one. Both grandparents mumbled, "Guess so," in tandem. When the kids moved she and Colin raised questioning eyebrows. But just before they did Tabby put her lips to Patti's ear and whispered.

"Hold his hand, Grammy. Suck it up and apologize even if it wasn't your fault."

~

Colin dragged the 'seen better days' tree from her garage to the living room. The kids had come up with a plan. Tabby found the box of worn ornaments in another cabinet. Braydon dug into it and pulled out tissue-wrapped curios.

"What's this one, Grammy?" His face paled. "Sorry. Is it okay I call you that.?"

Patti's eyes moistened. "Of course, Braydon. I am privileged. Thanks for the compliment."

He dropped the ornament on the coffee table and wrapped his arms around her waist. It felt so good to hug this child.

When they finally used all the old ornaments on the tree it didn't look so scraggly. It actually looked, as Tabby said, "Rather elegant."

Hot chocolate was next. Then Patti got an inspiration and pulled the cake mixes out of the pantry. She put out pans, muffin tins, bowls and stirrers and measuring cups. Lemon juice came next, then the gallon of OJ she'd bought the other day at Senior Day at Fry's market. She must have had a premonition. Everybody measured and dumped and stirred. They made ten cakes in her double ovens, and they smelled so good.

"Another sample, anyone?" She was scooping the last crumbs from one pan.

Tabby grabbed her elbow and pulled her into the guest bathroom. "Need to talk, Grammy."

Thirty

They were snuggled in old dog blankies in Patti's living room. A child held each of her hands. Braydon held hers and his grandpa's. Thank goodness the sofa was big so they all fit on it. The once scraggly tree lit up like, well, a proper Christmas tree. Fortunately, it had come with pre-lit lights, so no stringing lights had been necessary. A blessing of modern technology.

The ornament Braydon had questioned was the angel. It was the first one she and Devin had bought the first year they were married. It sat on the top of the uppermost branch.

Suddenly Tabby spoke up.

"Braydon and I want to share something Grammy and Mr. Colin. Something special."

All heads nodded. What, Patti wondered, could be more special on two days before Christmas Eve?

"We have decided to be a team." Tabby cocked her head for affirmation. When Braydon nodded, she continued.

"Bray has trouble with figuring out words sometimes. I have a lot of trouble with decimals." She nodded to him, he nodded back with a grin.

"So," she continued, "we will be helping each other. If you grandparents will approve us doing homework together at least once a week.

"Oh, almost forgot. I get the bonus. Braydon is going to teach me chess! I am so excited."

~

Colin grasped her hand clumsily. She wanted to tell him he squeezed too hard but didn't want to spoil the moment, if there was one. The two children were in her den on her computer. Not something she usually allowed, even with Tabby. But tonight was special. At least she hoped it was.

"Thinking about us," he said.

"What about us?"

"Dun know. Just thinking."

"And?"

"I really like you. More than like. Need more time, I guess."

"How much more time?" Was she pushing him too much? She squeezed back. Her hand was getting achy.

"Confused. Do you understand?"

"I do. But I can't wait forever."

"How long?"

"Don't know." But she was tempted to say "Whatever."

"Colin," she finally said, "maybe we should set a time. Like six months to get to know each other better. You okay with that?"

"Perfect. You are so clever, Patti."

She swallowed a smile. Six months would work. It would bring them to her birthday. Perfect time for a commitment. Maybe even a wedding.

Epilogue
Six Months Later

Patti adjusted her veil. A short headdress under a small tiara. She had not worn one for her marriage to Devin. Not a right choice for the time. She had always wanted to wear a sparkling crown, and Colin seemed to love the idea. Was it over the top for two marrying seniors? She didn't care. It was her wedding. So be it. She pressed her face to the mirror in the community center's rest room, thumbed her nose and laughed. "Whatever."

When she asked Colin for his opinion about wearing a tiara and veil at her age, he said, "Love the idea. Just so you marry me. Whatever."

Tabby was so excited. Too excited, Patti thought. "But," Tabby said defending herself, "I played cupid."

Patti knew she was right. If it hadn't been for the child's urging, she might not be standing here today ready to walk down the short aisle of the church's community center. Tabby wanted desperately to be in the wedding. She was too old to be a flower girl, a role usually dedicated to very young children who delighted in tossing petals.

Braydon, too, wanted to play an important role in the beginning of his grandpa's new life.

"I want to give you to Miss Patti, Gramps."

Colin was a bit abashed when Braydon started calling him Gramps, but he figured he knew where that had come from.

Both the bride and groom loved the idea of having their grandchildren in the ceremony. But because of their ages they were not old enough to sign the marriage certificate. Pastor Terry came up with the solution. Jennifer was the Maid of Honor and Caleb, the secret Santa who had almost fooled her, stood as Best Man to his twin brother. Tabitha got to wear a long, flowing green dress and carry a bouquet of Candy Cane roses from Patti's garden. Braydon clutched the rings in the pocket of his tuxedo jacket.

Patti and Colin had talked about marrying in their Santa and Mrs. Santa outfits for fun. Finally, they decided both wanted a more old-style wedding with traditional attire, yet reflecting how they met and their love for each other. Patti wore a "below the knee" gown and laughed that the phrase was a dress requirement in the Mrs. Santa contract. It was a lovely off-white gown embellished at the bodice and hem with red and green lace. Although difficult to find, Colin wore a pale-green tuxedo with a red vest and a rose boutonniere and a green and white fore-in-hand tie to complete the theme. He loved the idea of the tie since it was the knot he'd used first when learning how to tie a tie as a teen. Colin liked familiar, easy. Patti stuffed that in her memory bank and laughed. Would anything be easy for them?

Probably not, but life was exciting again. Besides, they had two smart grandkids to help them figure out life, and ties.

Patti was thrilled her Candy Cane roses were still blooming in the early Arizona summer heat. She fashioned a nosegay bouquet of them and tied them with the trim she cut off the silly Mrs. Santa bonnet. When she tossed the bonnet in the recycle bin she whispered "Whatever."

The teachers from the school had cleverly decorated the community center with holiday colors and Christmas ornaments to signify how the couple had met even though it was June and the ceremony was taking place on Patti's birthday. It was a perfect acknowledgement to honor them.

Just before the ceremony Tabitha pulled Patti aside.

"Figured out his problem, Grammy. He is color blind." Tabby looked at Patti with saucer eyes.

"Wha – what? How did you figure that out? How do you know?" Was she really having this conversation right before she walked down the aisle?

"I do a lot of internet research, Grammy. I'm almost positive. Not seeing the color blue of a word that says 'blue' in blue text, and seeing it as yellow or red, is very confusing."

Patti nodded. "We will figure this out. After," she repeated, "after Grandpa Colin and I get back from our honeymoon in Sedona."

"That's a beautiful place isn't it, Grammy? Supposed to be romantic."

"Yes, it is. But first we will travel Route 93 to

see Santa Land."

"What's that? Is it in Arizona?"

"Yes, it's abandoned. Has been for years. But we thought it would be fun to explore it . . . considering." Patti sighed thinking of all the adventures ahead. "Maybe next year we will go to Arrowhead, California to visit its Santa Village. For our anniversary." She realized Tabby had no clue about routes and highways. Why was she sharing this information?

"Sorry, Grammy. Wrong timing." Tabby stood on tiptoe and kissed Patti on her cheek. "Have a lovely love moon, or whatever it's called. I love you.

"Oh, there are glasses that can correct color blindness. Just thought you and my new Grandpa would want to know." She blew another kiss, picked up her rose bouquet and stood behind her mother to walk down the aisle.

Patti touched the diamond cross at her throat that Colin had given her and adjusted her short veil again. What would she, they, do without Tabby and Braydon? Maybe they never would have become friends or fallen in love as the legendary Christmas couple.

Glancing ahead she saw Colin's daughter Miranda, Braydon's mother, hair in place and coifed, standing tall and ginning. She turned and smiled catching Patti's eye. Miranda had finally understood how much Patti loved Braydon and just wanted to help. So many blessings.

The New Hope Community Church's praise band played *Here Comes Santa Claus* just as Patti took Colin's arm and they skipped down the red and green aisle together like two children enjoying life.

The End

Bonnie Engstrom loves Christmas and lives with
her own Santa of 55 years, even though he
complains about setting up the nine-foot tree every
year then loves putting the angel on top and stands
back to admire it. She and Dave are blessed to live
in Arizona with their two dogs and near four of their
six grandchildren. The other two live on the beach
in Costa Rica and surf. Pura Vida!

To see them all go to www.bonnieengstrom.com.

To connect with Bonnie visit her Facebook author
page where she has weekly contests to win books
and stash.
https://www.facebook.com/bonnieengstromauthor/.

Email her at bengstrom@hotmail.com and put
BOOKS in the subject line. She loves to chat with
readers.